UNDERLAND

A NOVEL

COLLEEN NELSON
and NANCY CHAPPELL-POLLACK

yellow dog

Yellow Dog
(an imprint of Great Plains Publications)
1173 Wolseley Avenue
Winnipeg, MB R3G 1H1
www.greatplains.mb.ca

Great Plains Publications gratefully acknowledges the financial support provided for its publishing program by the Government of Canada through the Canada Book Fund; the Canada Council for the Arts; the Province of Manitoba through the Book Publishing Tax Credit and the Book Publisher Marketing Assistance Program; and the Manitoba Arts Council.

Design & Typography by Relish New Brand Experience
Printed in Canada by Friesens

Library and Archives Canada Cataloguing in Publication

Title: Underland / Colleen Nelson and Nancy Chappell-Pollack.
Names: Nelson, Colleen, author. | Chappell-Pollack, Nancy, author.
Identifiers: Canadiana (print) 20200278134 | Canadiana (ebook) 20200278185 | ISBN 9781773370521 (softcover) | ISBN 9781773370538 (ebook)
Classification: LCC PS8627.E555 U53 2020 | DDC jC813/.6—dc23

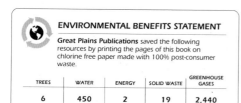

ENVIRONMENTAL BENEFITS STATEMENT

Great Plains Publications saved the following resources by printing the pages of this book on chlorine free paper made with 100% post-consumer waste.

TREES	WATER	ENERGY	SOLID WASTE	GREENHOUSE GASES
6	450	2	19	2,440
FULLY GROWN	GALLONS	MILLION BTUs	POUNDS	POUNDS

 Environmental impact estimates were made using the Environmental Paper Network Paper Calculator 4.0. For more information visit www.papercalculator.org.

Canadä

FSC
www.fsc.org
MIX
Paper from responsible sources
FSC® C016245

For Karen Deeley

Ama

I traced my finger over the lines gouged in the cave wall. As a youngun, I'd practised with a sharp stone till the wall was covered with my name. 'AMA' written a hundred times.

Jacob had taught letters to all the Unders who wanted to learn. He said living down here, we had to keep our minds sharp. Just because you live in a dark place doesn't make you dim, he said.

I've lived my whole life in the Underland, all twelve years. I knew that was my age because Jacob kept a tally chart on the cave wall. Before he went to sleep, he scratched a mark to keep track. "Keep track of what?" I asked once.

"How long I've been away from my people," he'd said. That was when Jacob started telling me his stories. About the Mountain, and outside.

He told me how before he and Noah were taken by the City people, time got marked by the sun. It woke up and fell asleep and that made a *day*. Those days got organized into weeks and months and seasons and then *years*. But in the Underland, there was no sun, so there weren't those other things either. All we knew was work and sleep. The tally helped Jacob to know things like how long he and Noah had been in the Underland, and how old some of us Unders were.

When a new youngun joined us, Jacob wrote their name over their mark on the wall. I found my 'AMA' marked over a clump of lines at the bottom. I counted all the way up till now and that was how I knew I was twelve. He marked other things on the cave wall too. Things Jacob said we had to remember, like when there was a cave-in and the names of the Unders we lost.

That was how it was down here. There was Big Mother who gave to us and Old Father who took when he got angry. Lila, who joked she was almost as old as the caves, said it like this: Old Father gets hungry. Same as we do. All this time, we take and take from him, digging and chipping at his insides. Well, sometimes he's gonna wanna take back to make up for what he lost.

Old Father scared me and every other Underlander and I tried my best not to make him mad.

As scared as us Unders were of Old Father, we loved Big Mother. She was everywhere and everything. She put new life inside the mothers, wherever they were. When a new youngun arrived, the nurses would show them off to us so we could see the pink-skinned freshness. A bright tender thing in all the darkness; a gift from Big Mother.

Jacob told me that where he lived before, babies came from mothers and fathers. Together they made a child and raised it together. He called it a *family*. In the Underland we were all family. The mothers and fathers couldn't be with their younguns, so we looked after each other.

Jacob and Noah were Prims before they came to live with us. They were different than the City people we dug for. The Prims didn't live under the dome. They lived on the Mountain. Jacob drew pictures on the walls with sharp stones to help me see it. The Mountain looked like the A in Ama. A stream wiggled over the land like a bug. There was a sun and it lit up *everything* and made things grow. Jacob told me people can't survive without the sun, which made me laugh because look at us Unders. We survive and we don't have a sun. Guess he was wrong about a few things.

Since I'd been a youngun, Lila had been filling my head with stories. She knew I was the one to carry them with me. "You see things other miss," she said to me one night. "You're a leader, Ama." I didn't know about that, but I liked that she'd picked me. She told me about Old Father and Big Mother and how us Unders came to be. Before we fell asleep, I told the stories out loud to anyone who wanted to listen. The words hung in the air so when we breathed them in, they became part of us. I missed hearing them from Lila's mouth, but I loved closing my eyes and letting them spill out, feeling those words wash over the walls and ground till we were scrubbed clean by them.

Romi was my best listener. She and I were like a split rock. Our two halves went together so perfect it was like we were one thing. She was the quiet and I was the loud. I was the hard and she was the soft. We were a little like Big Mother and Old Father that way. There couldn't be one of us without the other. When I was telling a story, it was Romi's face I watched the most. She drank up the words like they were water.

Jacob told me his stories too, so they'd carry on when he wasn't around. I soaked them up and made them mine, even though I'd never been on the Mountain. Noah caught him once, when I was six, telling me about the Mountain. His voice sounded like he was grinding rock dust between his teeth. "Why tell them about something they'll never see?"

Jacob stayed calm, like always, and said. "Maybe one day they will."

Noah snorted.

"You can't give up, Noah."

"Give up on what?" I asked.

"On getting out of here." That was the first time I heard about Jacob's plan to escape.

Sari

My stomach churned as I raised my hand to knock on Councillor Tar's door. I'd requested the meeting, but now that I was in the Underland, outside her chambers, I was second-guessing my decision. I had no idea how Tar would react when I told her the truth.

I'd been holding out hope that Kaia would return, but as the days stretched on, it was dwindling. She couldn't survive this long outside. It wasn't just the weather: if she'd made it to the Mountain, she'd have to deal with the threat of beasts and Prims. What if the information I'd hidden could help bring her back?

"Enter." I took a steadying breath. The most intimidating of the five Councillors, Tar's appearance and manner was harsh. Her voice was too—words came out like commands or criticisms. I opened the door and stepped inside her chambers. "Yes?"

Her scarlet robe stood out like a bloodstain against the bleakness of her chambers. I took a deep breath, steeling my nerve. After Kaia's disappearance had been noticed, I'd been interviewed by an overseer. I'd been honest about some things. I'd admitted to lying to our supervisor and covering for Kaia so she could grieve for Mae. It was a serious offense, and I'd lost a day's worth of joules as punishment.

But I'd kept other things secret, and now I wondered if that had been the right choice. Back in my dwelling, I'd rehearsed what I'd say to Tar, but now that I was across from her, it was more nerve-wracking than I expected. "I have some information about Kaia."

Tar gestured for me to sit. My tunic pinched at my neck. Had it always been this tight? Or had Tar's imperious gaze made my clothes shrink? I rubbed my thumb over the spot on my finger where the pulse point had been implanted at birth. A monitor, tracking device and communicator all in one, it gave the Councillors and overseers access to a Citizen's every movement.

"Tell me," Tar prompted.

"Before Kaia left, her pulse point malfunctioned."

Tar's eyes bored into me. "How long before?"

"A few days. She kept it a secret because of Mae. She was energy sharing with her to delay her balancing." Which had backfired. Mae had been taken anyway, and that had started the whole terrible chain of events that had landed me here, in front of Tar.

Tar's fingers curled into a fist. "Was her locator working?"

I shook my head. "No. Nothing worked. Her communicator was broken too."

"Why are you telling me this now?"

I'd been as shocked as anyone when the news alert had gone out that a Citizen was missing. When I realized it was my best friend, it had felt like the ground had given way. There were rumours that she'd been taken by a Prim or was hiding somewhere in the City. But then it was revealed that overseers, including Lev, Tar's offspring and my mate, had been sent out to bring her back.

The City had been in a holding pattern since then, waiting for her to return. "I thought she'd come back on her own."

"And now you're worried keeping her secret has cost you your best friend," Tar guessed.

I nodded, miserable. The truth was I'd lost her before she even left the City. Matching with Lev had made sure of that.

"Even if Kaia's pulse point was working, it wouldn't help us find her. They don't work once a Citizen leaves the City. Why do you think Lev hasn't come back? We have no way to communicate with him."

The last bit of hope leaked out of me. Keeping Kaia's secret hadn't hurt her, but it wasn't going to help her either.

"Did she ever talk about leaving?" Tar asked, leaning forward.
I shook my head. "Never."

"And in the days before she left, did she seem different to you?"

"Yes, I mean, she'd lost her elder. She didn't take it well."
Citizens were supposed to be logical about the need for balancings. They happened all the time and kept the City sustainable.
Kaia could have celebrated Mae's long life. Instead, she'd let Mae's death eat away at her. She'd holed up in her capsule for days. Maybe I shouldn't have been surprised; after all, she'd been confiding in me about her birth elder's unpredictable moods for years. Maybe more of Sy's instability had slipped into her DNA than I thought. "My match with Lev didn't help."

I wanted to believe it was Mae's balancing that pushed Kaia to leave, but deep down I knew my union with Lev had been the tipping point. We'd left her with no one to turn to. She believed her best friends had betrayed her. That *I* had betrayed her. "I never should have agreed to it."

Tar narrowed her eyes at me. "You made a decision that benefitted your future. No one could fault you for that."

"Kaia did."

Tar looked at me, considering something. Prickles of sweat broke out on the back of my neck. Being on the receiving end of Tar's unforgiving gaze was the last place I wanted to be. "Before I allowed you to match with Lev, I checked your personality profile. You scored high in moral ambiguity. What's interesting about that is that I did too." She arched an eyebrow. The idea that Tar and I had anything in common was hard to believe. She was the most powerful person in the City; Citizens feared her.

"Do you know what that means?"

I shook my head.

"All strong leaders need moral ambiguity. It gives us the freedom to make hard decisions. We see the end game and we're not concerned with who we step on to get there." Her lips stretched into a smile. "I want you to know, I understand you. Better than you think."

I stared at Tar. She thought I was like her, a leader. I was too stunned to say anything. I was *nothing* like her.

"I could help you become someone in the City. Maybe even a Councillor one day. You're matched with my offspring; it would be natural for me to mentor you."

My breath caught in my throat at her offer. It wasn't something I had ever considered.

"Think about it," she said.

"I—I will," I stammered.

As I left her chambers and made my way back to work, Tar's offer echoed in my head. For a few minutes, thinking about what it would it be like to wield a Councillor's power was a pleasant distraction. Citizens nodded in deference and moved out of the way when they strode down the walkways. The five Councillors made decisions that affected all our lives. They ran the City. Nothing happened that didn't have their approval. But by the time I got back to work at the fetal assessment clinic, reality set in.

My quest for status was why I was in this predicament in the first place. I'd agreed to match with Lev, and it had cost me my best friend. I had to learn to be content with what I had.

Ama

Long ago, a city got built. It had a dome and could protect all the people that lived inside it. It had an underground too, and diggers were needed to tunnel deep into the earth. The work was hard and the men who got recruited were strong. When the city was finished, the people who ran it didn't want to let them go; they were needed for something else now. 'We have a new job for you,' the City people said.

'We need you to dig for what will keep the City running, for the brine that is buried underground.'
But the men didn't want to dig anymore. They were ready to go back to their families; they missed their children and wives. The City people had an idea. They'd bring the children and wives to them. Now the men wouldn't need to leave because they'd all be together.
The men agreed because they thought they'd get to live up above, under the dome; their families would be safe, and they'd all be together. But the City people had a different plan. They wanted to keep the men underground, so they did.
The men didn't like being cheated. There was an ugly battle and an unfair fight. The men who survived were taken away. No one saw them again. But now, the City people didn't have anyone to dig so they came up with a different plan. Underland children would be taught to do the job their fathers had done. They might not be as strong, but children are smaller, they can fit through tight tunnels. Children are nimble and quick and don't fight back.
That is how us Unders came to be.

I scratched a little line on the cave wall, another mark for another shift. It used to be Jacob's job to do this, but since he was gone, it fell on me. I'd put an X above the line when he got taken. That was fifteen sleeps ago. I swallowed hard and walked away from the wall.

"Coming, Ama?" Kibo called. The leader of my team, he was the one we followed into the tunnels. A long line of us, fifty Unders in all, snaked past the rock we called Big Mother. It dangled down from the ceiling of the cave, glistening silvery white. It had a lump in the middle that looked like a belly, which was why we called it Big Mother. She'd been there for who knows how long watching over us. No matter how mad Old Father got or how bad he made the walls tremble, Big Mother didn't budge.

After I whispered a prayer to Big Mother asking her to keep us safe, I caught up with my team and went into the tunnels. Each team branched off toward a different digging chamber. I adjusted the rope that crisscrossed my chest. Attached to it was the basket that was used to carry the brine from the digging chamber to the conveyor belt. After muling for so long, the skin under my tunic was thick with calluses. All the mules had scars from where the ropes had rubbed the skin raw. Our knees and hands were all chewed up from crawling, our faces, arms, and legs coated with dirt.

Diggers didn't have it any better. On my team, Kibo and Abel had swollen hands. The skin on their palms was as tough as that on their feet. Muscles bulged across their aching backs because they spent every shift chipping at the walls of Old Father with dull axes. *Tch tch tch.* We heard that sound in our sleep. It echoed till the rock hummed with it.

Each of us had a headlamp that was strapped to our head and powered by our body heat. The more we dug or the faster we crawled, the brighter it shone.

Us Unders dug for the brine the City people needed to keep everything running. Brine came out of the rock walls in glittering chunks. Once the diggers had a pile, mules like me carried it in baskets on our backs to the depot. Jacob and Noah said on the Mountain it was called *salt*.

"Ama," Kibo called me over, his voice echoed off the walls. Kibo had wispy bits of curly hair that grew in tufts all over his head and eyes that bugged out a little. His ears stuck out too, like mine, but Kibo can wiggle his; I can't. Sometimes he gave my ears a tweak, to remind me.

The pile of glittering brine crystals lay at his feet. Behind him, grimy with rock dust, was Abel. So quiet sometimes we forgot he was there, he kept chipping at the rock as Kibo loaded his pile into my basket. He was gentle, like if he put the brine in softly it wouldn't weigh as much.

When I had taken all I could, the pile was only half gone. "Luken," Kibo said. "Come here."

Luken was the new mule I was training. He was young and small, too small to be muling, if you asked me. "I can take more," I said.

Kibo frowned. "He's got to take his fair share. It's the only way he'll get strong."

"It's his third shift. Third's the hardest, everyone knows that. He can get strong on his fourth shift." Kibo, even though he was older than me by two years, knew better than to argue. I could be hard as rock when I wanted to be.

Once the basket was loaded up, I checked for balance, making sure none of the brine was gonna fall out of it in the tunnels. "I can take a little more," I said.

Instead, Kibo tweaked my ear. "You have enough. Luken will be right behind you."

I nodded and crawled across the stone floor to the tunnel opening. As soon as I got into the tunnel, I had to crouch down so I didn't bump my head. There wasn't much clearance for my basket of brine, which was why only small kids like me could be mules. A basket like this on Kibo would have meant he'd be crawling on his belly. As it was, getting him in and out of the tunnels was becoming tricky. He'd gotten stuck once a few shifts ago. His shoulders were too broad to fit and he'd had to wiggle like a bug to get free.

I went slow, waiting on Luken to catch up. "Ama?" he called.

"I'm here," I said impatiently. If I closed my eyes, I could smell him, his scent loud against the damp walls. He'd have to learn to do that too. None of us Unders could rely on our eyes in the dark tunnels. It was our noses that helped the most. And ears too, I guess. But it was easier to tell people apart by their smell than the sound of their breathing.

The tunnel we were in led to the depot. The Unders on cranker duty used pulleys to send the brine somewhere else. "We're almost there, Luken." I was moving slow, so the headlamp's glow was too weak to do any good. "You have to pay attention to the path so you can find it on your own," I told him.

When we got to the depot, the crankers helped Luken dump his basket of brine into the big bucket that got heaved up somewhere else.

Luken tugged at the ropes crisscrossing his chest. Empty now, the basket flopped. "I want to take it off." His voice cracked and I knew tears weren't far behind.

"No. All that's gonna do is make the hurt worse when you have to put it back on. The best way is if the skin hardens. You gotta get scars for that to happen. We'll get Lila to put on the healing mud when we're in the pit."

"Ama," someone called. I didn't need to sniff the air to know who it was. Romi appeared from a different tunnel, her basket filled with half the amount of brine I'd carried. She murmured words of encouragement to Luken and I wished Noah had given Luken to Romi to train. She was better with the younguns than I was.

"How's the digging?" I asked. It was a common question in the Underland. We all wanted to know where good amounts of brine were found. It would tell us the direction that new tunnels would need to be dug.

"Our hole's almost empty."

"Ours too." The crankers helped unload Romi's basket. We were about to head back down the tunnels when the crankers called for us to stop. A bucket of food had been lowered, which meant it was quitting time. The bucket came down once a day.

The nutritional mix would be combined with water from the pool into a sludge that was the consistency of wet mud and tasted about the same, except salty on account of the briny water. Sometimes we'd get bonuses. Limp, leafy green things that Jacob said was kale.

"We're done," I said, turning to Luken.

He fell against my gritty body like he was going to collapse.

"Come on," I said. "We still gotta get back to the pit." Romi shot me a look. I rolled my eyes at her but crouched down so I was nose to nose with Luken. "Look," I said, as patiently as I could, "Every day it's gonna get easier. I promise. Before you know it, you'll be the one training a youngun."

"It's never gonna get easier." Tears glistened in his eyes, but I shook my head.

"Don't start crying, Luken," I said, irritated. "If Krux is in the pit and sees you crying, he'll think you're weak. He'll send you." Luken's chin quivered, but the tears wobbling in his eyes never fell.

I hated having to scare him, but what I'd said was the truth.

"I don't like Krux," Luken whispered.

"None of us do," I agreed. Krux was a City person and the only one of them who ever came into the pit. We were all scared of him, even Jacob and Noah. He carried a zapper stick to sizzle anyone who didn't listen, but that wasn't what I was afraid of. It was his eyes.

They were pale and he hardly blinked, so when he found someone he was interested in, his eyes stuck and didn't let go. Whenever he came to the pit, I worried his eyes were gonna find me or Romi. Thinking about what would happen if they did sent a jolt through me worse than what his zapper could do.

Noah and Jacob called Krux the Boss. He decided who went where in the Underland. He'd sent Luken out of the nest to start muling and he'd decide which of the mules were strong enough to start digging. Krux was also looking for Unders who got sickly and couldn't work anymore. When a boy got to being a man, Krux told them they were ready to live with Old Father. It was an exciting time for the boys. We clapped them out as they left with Krux, shouting goodbye till the rocks sang with us. It wasn't the same for the girls. When one of us left to join Big Mother, there was no loud cheering. The weight of what she'd been chosen to do was too important. Krux kept an eye on us, looking for the few girls who were fleshy in the right parts and got their bleeds. Only some girls were special enough to be blessed by Big Mother. I just hoped I wasn't one of them. As much as I wanted to rest my aching body, I wasn't going anywhere without Romi. Once you left the pit, boy or girl, you didn't come back.

Maybe I'd end up like Lila. She'd never left the pit because her bleeds never came. She said she prayed to Big Mother to send them, but nothing happened. In the end, she thinks Big Mother knew letting her stay in the pit was the right thing. Even though she couldn't be a mother, she raised the ones who would be.

"Will you tell me a story later?" Luken asked as we made our way through the tunnels to the pit.

The pit was the biggest space in the Underland, and it was where we ate and slept. It had a high, domed ceiling. Smaller chambers led off of it. One of them was the pool and another, the nest, where the younguns and their nurses slept.

"Maybe," I said with a sigh. Those first sleeps in the pit had been hard on Luken. Without the crush of other bodies around him, he'd wept and shivered alone on his mat. Finally, Romi had convinced me to let him crawl over to ours. I'd whispered a story in his ear till he drifted off. I never should have let Romi talk me into it though. Now he expected one before every sleep.

The glare of big light blinded me when we stepped out of the dark tunnels and into the pit. Big light worked when an Under cranked a pedal with their feet. It illuminated almost all the pit.

As soon as my eyes adjusted, I scanned the pit for Jacob, hoping he'd be there. But it was Noah doing head count, and everyone wore the same dreary expression. If Jacob had returned, there'd be celebrating. Since Krux had come to take him, we'd all been on edge. No one knew why or where he'd gone, or if he was ever coming back. Beside me, Luken tore at the ropes. I slapped his hands away. "Fighting only makes the knots tighter." I untied them and he sighed with relief when they fell to the cave floor. "Take off your shirt," I said. He pulled it off, trying not to let the rough fabric rub against his torn-up skin. Blood oozed where the ropes had been. "Get to Lila," I told him. She was sitting on her mat in the center of the pit, surrounded by the remedies and supplies Krux gave her to keep us healthy.

"Come," he said and pulled my hand.

"She's right there," I pointed across the pit. "I'll watch you, but you have to go on your own." He didn't move. *Stubborn youngun*, I thought. I got busy taking off my basket and stretching my back, watching him out of the corner of my eye to see if he went. "If you wait too long, there's gonna be a lineup of people who need Lila's help." I told him. "You better go."

Pouting, he walked across the pit. I kept my eye on him till he got there and went to get the food. I had just sat down when Luken came back with one of Lila's clay bowls filled to the top with her special mud. "She said you were supposed to put it on me."

"Sit down," I told him. "We gotta get this on before it dries out." The sores were worse than I thought, but the mud was cool and slick. He gasped as I smoothed it on over his back and chest. "You'll feel better after a sleep," I said. "I'll put some bandages on before your next shift," I promised him. "It'll help."

"Thank you, Ama," he said when I was done.

"Now, you eat and then sleep." I passed him his bowl of food and a gourd of water.

He gave me a shy look. "Can I sleep with you?"

I shook my head. "No. You gotta learn to sleep on your own."

"But Romi sleeps with you."

"That's different."

"Why?"

"It just is."

His lip quivered. I knew Kibo was right about him toughening up, but the same reason I'd taken part of his load to the depot made me say, "I'll stay with you on your mat till you're asleep. How's that?"

I ignored the eye roll Romi gave me when she found me later with Luken's head on my lap. "I don't know why you act so tough with him. You're just a softie, same as me," she said, sitting beside me.

"I never saw anyone fall asleep so fast," I said to her. My hand had strayed to his hair, a matted mess.

"He's too little to be muling. How old do you think he is?" Romi asked.

I knew exactly how old he was. Luken's name was on Jacob's wall. "He's four."

She shook her head. "Krux must have been desperate if he took him from the nest when he's so young."

The things Krux did were a mystery to all of us Unders. "If Jacob had been here, he wouldn't have let it happen." Thinking about Jacob made my chest tighten. We lost people down here all the time. Between cave-ins, sickness or people getting sent, none of us were strangers to missing someone, but I more than missed Jacob. It was like part of me was lost.

Luken didn't stir when I moved his head off my lap and stood up. "I thought he'd be back by now," I whispered as Romi and I walked across the pit to our mat. I'd worked up the courage to ask Noah, but my question had received a sullen response, just like I'd expected. Since Jacob had left, Noah was gripped in his gloominess. All us Unders avoided him, which was easy. He sat at his station raised up from the rest of us and stared down at the pit, his mind somewhere else.

"Do you think Krux found out about—" she gave a chin nod toward the pool. Despite her voice being just a whisper, I stiffened and hushed her. "No one can hear," she said.

Even though our mat was at the far end of the pit, barely touched by big light's glare, I glanced around nervously. "If Krux had found out, we'd all have felt his zapper stick." The digging Jacob and I were doing was secret. Romi and Noah were the only other people who knew about it. When every other Under was sleeping, me and Jacob would sneak to the cranny by the pool and dig. We chipped away at the rock, letting it fall down the tunnel into the pool so there'd be no evidence for Krux to find. Before he got taken, Jacob figured we were close to breaking through to the surface.

"What if Jacob left without us? What if he got a chance and took it?"

I narrowed my eyes at Romi, angry that she'd even think that. "Jacob would never do that. Anyhow, you saw Krux take him. He didn't leave because he wanted to."

"It was just a thought," she muttered and lay down on the mat. She rolled over and put her back to me. I wiggled around. The thin mat did nothing to soften the cave floor. I listened as Romi's breath grew deeper. She'd drifted off quickly while I lay stewing about Jacob. Was she right? Had Jacob found a way to escape and taken it?

And if he had, was he coming back to get us?

Sari

The fetal assessment clinic was busy. Without Kaia, we were one technician short. I should have been reading scans, but instead, my mind was elsewhere. Not on Tar's offer to be her protégé—I'd pushed that from my head already. She'd misread my agreement to match with Lev for ambition. I'd wanted status, that was true, but I had no interest in the kind of power she wielded. With a few minutes between patients, I projected my hologram in the air in front of me. I swiped left and all my work files appeared.

We weren't supposed to open inactive files, but my clearance gave me access to them. Every so often, I'd take a peek at the genetic material of someone I knew. I'd never looked at Kaia's before. Why would I? She was my best friend. I knew everything about her, or at least I thought I did.

I'd been thinking more and more about how shocking it was that she'd left the City. Tar had asked if she'd ever talked about it before. I'd answered no because she was my best friend and had never mentioned leaving. We talked about everything, or we had up until she'd left. What if she'd been hiding more of Sy's genetics than she let on? I knew how his moods affected him, did Kaia share the same predilection? Could that have pushed her to leave?

To find Kaia's records, I first had to search for the numeric code that identified her DNA. Every citizen was catalogued this way. We were numbers before we were ever humans. There she was: 98340087. A beautiful double helix of chromosomes. I took a closer look, running my eyes down the list of genetic sequencing. It was the same thing I did for every test we ran on a newly implanted embryo. Nothing was out of place. I swiped to the next page in her file.

It was a listing of her birth elders. All the pertinent information about Raina and Sy. Raina's was all normal. Above average intelligence, a surgeon, fertile. I moved on to Sy's. It also looked unremarkable until I took noticed an asterisk in the column under offspring. What did that mean?

"Sari," my supervisor said as she walked into my cubicle. I tucked my finger away and the hologram vanished. She pursed her lips. Her disapproval was plain. "Your next appointment's here."

"Thanks," I said and waited till she'd left before pulling up the file again. I scrolled down. At the bottom of the file was the asterisk and one word: Intertwining.

What was intertwining?

"Sari!" My supervisor's voice sliced through my thoughts.

"Send her in," I called. For the rest of my shift, I went through the motions of scanning and reassuring the pregnant females, but in my head, one word kept repeating.

Intertwining.

⁀

I stared at the door in front of me. How many times had I come here, or called up to Kaia from the walkway beneath her balcony? I'd never hesitated before. But I'd always known that Kaia, or Mae, would be on the other side of the door. Sy too, but he wasn't someone I ever looked forward to seeing. He'd always been distant, preferring digging in the garden to spending time with people.

I did a quick rap, three times, and waited. No answer. I hadn't come to console him, but with a pang of guilt, I realized I should have visited before. I'd been so wrapped up in my loss, it hadn't occurred to me that Sy was missing Kaia and Mae, the same as me. I knocked again and stood waiting. "That dwelling is empty."

A voice from behind startled me. I turned around. "Ren!" He'd been in my class at school and looked as surprised to see

me as I was to see him. He was in his overseer uniform. The
collar sat high on his neck; the stiff fabric stretched across his
shoulders.

"Sari! I thought it was you. You cut your hair."

I ran a hand through it self-consciously. After letting my hair
grow and hoping its length would give me an edge when I put
my name in for a mate, I'd chopped it off when Lev and I had
matched. Dark blond, it was longer in the front and swooped
over my forehead. The back had been shaved to my scalp and
had grown out. It was still soft to the touch.

"What are you doing here?"

I nodded at the door. "This was Kaia's dwelling. I was looking
for Sy, her birth elder."

At the mention of Kaia's name, Ren's face fell. "I'm sorry
about Kaia. You were close with her, weren't you? I often saw
you together at the gymnasium."

"Very close. She was my best friend," I admitted. "I thought
I should check on Sy. See how he's doing."

Ren frowned. "He doesn't live here anymore."

"Oh." I can't say I was surprised. One person in a dwelling meant for three was unusual. "Do you know where he was
moved to."

"I do. Um," he fidgeted, clearly uncomfortable with the topic.
"He was taken to be balanced."

Sy's death didn't hit me the same as losing Kaia, or Mae, but
it was still sad. Everyone close to Kaia except for me was gone.
And so were my hopes of finding out what 'Intertwining' meant.

"I didn't hear about it," I said, confused. Usually, balancings were
announced ahead of time so Citizens could celebrate a life well
lived with the about-to-be-balanced Citizen. Mae had been taken
so suddenly; she'd been robbed of a final goodbye. It was one of
the reasons Kaia had had such a hard time with her death.

Ren hesitated, glanced in each direction and then said, "He's still being held actually. There's a problem with the crop of bane-berries. A delay. It happens sometimes."

"He's still alive."

Ren nodded.

"Could I see him? To say goodbye?"

Ren shook his head and was about to say no. I couldn't let this chance slip through my fingers. I let a swath of hair fall over one eye and looked up at him, pleadingly. "It would mean a lot to me. The last few weeks have been hard."

He relented. "I'll see what I can do. I can send you a message."

I gave him a grateful smile. "Thank you." I held up my index finger. Ren pressed the soft pad of his fingertip against mine. "Contact data. Ren. Accepted," said my communicator.

"I'll wait to hear from you," I said and turned to go. I kept my steps light in case he was still watching me. Kaia would not have disappeared from the City without telling me. If she'd left, there had been a reason for it, and I needed to know what it was.

Ama

Luken said that the fourth work shift had been worse than the third. The mud from Lila had helped though, so had the bandages I'd wrapped around his torso. I tried to tell all that to Romi as we lay on our mat at sleep time. There was something different about her. I'd felt it since she came out of the tunnel. A different smell too, like her, but riper. "You're not even listening to me," I said to her.

"I am," she sighed.

I knew Romi's face and her smell and how her skin felt better than I knew my own. Since we were younguns, Romi and I fell asleep with our noses pressed together, breathing each other's air.

Knowing her as well as I did, I knew she was hiding something. "What's wrong?" I asked.

Her voice came, thin as a ripple. "I started my bleeds."

I sat up and rolled her over, so I was staring at her face. In the dark, all I could see were her eyes glistening. "When?"

"We were in the tunnels. My stomach started to ache, like it was being squeezed. I checked and then I knew why."

I lay back down and stared up into the dark. My chest got heavy, like someone was sitting on it.

"What's it like?" I whispered.

"Achy. Lila said the bleeds will get heavier next time." It wasn't the bleeding I was worried about. Now that they'd started, it meant Romi could be a mother. Krux could take her away. For the first time in our lives, we'd be apart. What if my bleeds never came? I reached out for Romi's hand and laced my fingers through hers, like my grip could keep her close.

"I'm scared, Ama."

I was too, but I didn't want Romi to know that. "The tunnel is almost finished. Soon as it is, we're leaving," I promised.

"What if it's too late?" she asked. "What if I'm already a mother?" None of us, not even Lila, knew where the mothers went. Us older Unders grilled the younguns trying to find out what they remembered about their time with them, but we never got much. The only one who knew where the mothers were was Krux.

"If Krux takes me, will you come find me?" Romi asked.

I hated hearing her talk like that. "He's not going to—"

"Ama," she said, as if I were a youngun, "we both know it's gonna happen, sooner or later."

I looked down at my chest. Flat. Hips still too narrow. Romi's curves had started. Now that she had her bleeds, it was only a matter of time until Krux noticed. "I wish my bleeds would start. Then we'd be together."

"Don't say that. You have to stay. How are we gonna escape if you're a mother?"

I took a deep breath, trying to keep my thoughts straight. I wished Jacob were here to make sense of things for me.

I stood up.

"Where are you going?"

"To dig," I whispered.

"Without Jacob?" She couldn't see me nod in the dark.

I bent down close to her. She opened her mouth to say something else, but I put my lips on hers and pressed them hard. We'd been together our whole lives, but the way I kissed her this time was different. I didn't want to stop. The warmth of her kissing me back went right down into my belly. Finally, I pulled away.

Neither of us said anything. We didn't need to. That was how it was with me and Romi. I kept that warmth from her mouth as I tiptoed along the cave wall towards the pool. My feet knew the way on their own. Almost every night for six years, I'd been meeting Jacob there; the two of us digging and waiting for the right moment to share our plan with the rest of the Unders.

Sari

Ren didn't waste any time. I got a message to meet him before work at the entrance to the Underland. There could only be one reason: he'd found a way to get me in to see Sy. On my way, I stopped at the market and bought him an orange. The fruit seller picked one and held it to me like a prize. "Five joules."

Five was steep. I glanced at the numbers that glowed through my skin. I hadn't gone to the gymnasium last night and my joules were running low. "Three," I said firmly.

The orange probably came from a tree on his balcony, although some people in the market supplemented their stock with nighttime visits to the orchard—a punishable offense if they got caught. "Fine, three," he said and nodded. I transferred the joules to him. Instantly the number that glowed through the skin on my finger decreased. As promised, Ren was waiting at the stairs to the Underland. I held out the orange with a smile and a flourish. "What's this?" he asked.

"A thank you gift."

"I'm not used to getting gifts," he said and tossed it hand to hand. "Perhaps we can enjoy it together at lunch?"

Before my match with Lev, I would have jumped at the chance. Ren was everything I wanted in a mate, including the offspring of a Councillor. "I can't," I said.

Ren winced with embarrassment. "Of course. I'm sorry. It was stupid of me. I forgot."

"I forget sometimes too," I admitted. "He hadn't even moved into our dwelling before he left."

"Don't give up hope," Ren said. "Raf went with him and he's one of the strongest overseers we have."

I glanced at Ren. His sincerity caught me by surprise. With Kaia gone, I had no one to confide in. My birth elders were basically strangers and I'd never been close to Mika, my birth sibling, and now she was wrapped up in her own life. Tears sprang to my eyes. Emotions weren't something Citizens showed to others. I turned away. I didn't want to make Ren uncomfortable. "I want to believe that, but it's been so long."

With all the dangers outside, why would Kaia have chosen to leave? More and more, I was sure something else had pushed her to go. Sy might be the only one who could give me the answers I needed. I cleared my throat and took a determined breath. It was now or never. "We should go," I said.

"Are you sure?"

I nodded. "I'm ready."

The Underland was a maze of tunnels and large corridors that wound their way beneath the City. There were private chambers for Councillors, workspaces, and storage rooms. We passed other overseers, but none of them gave me a second look since I was with Ren. "When we get to his cell, you'll only have a few minutes." I didn't know what I was going to say to Sy. All my thoughts were jumbled, and Ren's lunch invitation hadn't helped. "Thank you," I said to him when we were alone in the corridor. "I know you're not supposed to be doing this."

He gave me a weighty look and dropped his voice. "Krux says the baneberries won't be ripe for at least another week. Maybe longer."

Krux. Even hearing the name of the citizen responsible for balancings sent a shiver down my spine. As the City's balancer, he was responsible for mercifully killing those who could no longer produce enough energy to survive. Overseers brought the elders to him and he fed them juice from the white baneberries, which were grown in a secret lab far away from the rest of our crops. The poison spread through them and their death would happen quickly and painlessly.

"So he'll be in a cell until then?"

Ren nodded. "He's not the only one. There's another elder too." The arch of his eyebrow told me he didn't agree with imprisoning them.

I looked at Ren. He was saying things unusual for someone in his job. "You don't seem like an overseer."

"I'll take that as a compliment." There was no mistaking the rueful tone of his voice.

"Good. That's how I meant it," I said truthfully.

"Overseeing wasn't my first choice. My birth elder pulled some strings, which is how I ended up down here." Lots of offspring secured their positions thanks to their elders' connections. That's how Lev had ended up as an overseer too.

As we walked, the air grew musty and smelled of damp earth. A series of cutouts in the ceiling allowed light from the City above to filter through. Eventually, the cutouts disappeared as the corridor sloped downward. Ren gripped the handle of his lightstick. The bulb glowed, powered by his body's energy. At this time of day, the City would be bathed in light. But in the Underland, it could have been midnight. I stuck close to Ren and wondered how much farther we had to go.

Ren stopped outside a door blocked by many bamboo poles lashed together with twine. I hugged my arms trying to fend off the chill of the Underland and winced at the thought of Sy being trapped behind the door.

Ren held out the lightstick to me. "You have to go in by yourself. I'll wait out here and keep watch." I took the lightstick and it momentarily dulled, then glowed brightly as my clammy palms closed around the handle.

He heaved open the door. I took a step forward. The cell was small. A quick sweep of the lightstick and all four walls were visible, little more than an arm's length away. The human stink made my eyes water. Behind me, the door shut.

Sy didn't look up when I walked in. He was curled in a corner, scratching his nail into the dirt walls. His long legs were tucked under him, the frayed tunic exposed his bony ankles and shins. I wasn't prepared for this. Sy was not well.

The lightstick flickered as I adjusted my grip on it. Holding it tighter than I needed to, it surged with my anxious energy.

"Sy?" I said. "It's Sari." His finger stopped moving for a second, but he didn't look my way. His face was discoloured with bruising, some old and some fresh. There was a cut across the bridge of his nose. Ren hadn't mentioned it had taken violence to get him here.

"Sari," he whispered, staring at the wall.

I swallowed. It was like he was in another world. Slowly, I made my way closer to him and crouched down. "How are you, Sy?" He made no movement to show he'd heard me. I swallowed nervously. "Kaia's gone. Did you know?" He mumbled something unintelligible. I pressed on. "I miss her. I want her to come home." He'd stopped scratching the wall and sat motionless. I realized the marks on the wall weren't just gouges, they were stained with blood too. He'd worn away the tip of his finger making the markings. I didn't know how much longer I had in the cell. If I was going to ask about what I'd seen in Kaia's file, I'd have to do it now. "Sy," I said gently, "I looked at Kaia's file. Something didn't make sense." *Tread carefully*, I warned myself. "There was a word I'd never seen before. Maybe you know what it is." I paused.

He looked at me, waiting.

"The word was intertwining."

His sudden movement took me by surprise. In a flash he was up and across the room, pulling me to my feet. His fingers dug into the soft spot below my collarbone.

I screamed. He pushed me back against the wall, knocking the wind out of me. The lightstick slipped out of my hands and fell to the ground. The light died and we were plunged into darkness. "You're working with them!" he shouted in my face.

"No!" I gasped. Sy's fingertips were slippery with blood as they found their way to my windpipe.

"I found it on her file," I gurgled.

As suddenly as he'd grabbed me, he let go. I coughed and gasped for breath. I went to the ground, slapping the floor frantically for the lightstick. My hands closed around the cylinder and as soon as I held it the light glowed.

Sy was lucid now, I could see it in his eyes. Even with his stooped shoulders, when he stood at his full height, he towered over me. "What does it mean?" I asked again.

"Why do you care? She's gone and she's not coming back."

"She's my best friend. I want to know what happened, and if it's"—the next part was hard to say out loud—"if it's my fault she left."

Sy grumbled and narrowed his eyes at me. "Because you matched with Lev, you mean?"

I nodded warily. I'd believed Tar when she'd told me they'd never be together. I'd been desperate and when Tar had dangled an ideal match in front of me, I'd snatched it. "I didn't mean to hurt her," I said.

Sy surveyed me and I forced myself to hold his gaze. Finally, he spoke. "Kaia left the City to find her birth elder."

"Raina?" I asked. That didn't make any sense. Raina was dead. I sighed. The days in the cell had broken Sy and left him a shell of a person. Trying to get answers from him had been a waste of time. "She died, Sy. A long time ago." Kaia had been a toddler. She had no memory of Raina.

He shook his head. "Raina escaped. I helped her just like I helped Kaia."

I gave Sy a sharp look. "What do you mean? How?"

Sy smirked. "No one wants to remember the past. What it took to build the City. The sacrifice. So the truth lies buried in the Underland."

"What are you talking about?" I didn't have time for riddles.

"You want to know about intertwining? Then you have to go deeper."

"Deeper where?"

He turned to the corner of the room he'd been sitting in when I arrived. "Into the pit. That's where the answers are."

I wanted to scream in frustration. "Sy, tell me what you mean. Please. I don't have much time."

He came at me again. This time, I was ready. I swung at

him with the lightstick, but missed. He lunged, pinning me back against the wall with his arm. With his free hand, he unpeeled my fingers from the lightstick. "Ren!" I called, but my voice was weak with fear. The pressure of his arm made it hard take a breath. Sy's hot breath exploded in my face. It stank and I turned away. He was going to kill me. In this cell, with an overseer not a metre away in the corridor. "Ren!" I tried again.

"Listen to me," he whispered. He'd managed to get my index finger free and pressed the bloody tip of his pulse point against mine. I struggled, desperate to free myself. He had more strength than I thought possible. "You can find the truth yourself. I've given you everything you need."

"Data transfer complete." My eyes flared open at the communicator's voice in my ear.

"What have you done?"

"Given you the answers. It's too late to help Kaia. Maybe you can save yourself." I shuddered as Sy fell away from me. I had the lightstick firmly in my hand again.

"Ren!" I shouted. My voice shook. "Ren!" I kept the beam of light on Sy as he stumbled back to the mattress. Just as when I'd arrived, he lifted his hand and began scratching against the wall. I could see now, it wasn't just random marks, as I'd first thought. Sy was writing a word: Jacob.

"Who is Jacob?" I asked. In the corridor, I could hear the bar sliding back. In a second, Ren would open the door. "Sy! Why are you writing that name?"

He ran his fingers over it tenderly. "Follow the map and you'll see." His voice drifted off.

"What map?"

But it was pointless, he was lost to me again.

Ama

When I left our sleeping mat, I didn't go straight to the cranny that hid our escape tunnel. First, I stopped at Big Mother. The rock was slick and cool like always. I put a hand on the lump that was shaped like a full belly and thought about Romi. *Please don't let Krux take her. Not yet.* I rested my forehead against her and wrapped my arms around her bulging middle. I imagined Big Mother hugging me back, telling me in her way that everything was going to be okay.

Just past Big Mother was the pool. Even without a headlamp, I could see that it shimmered. Little glow bugs stuck to the ceiling and lit up the darkness with a yellowish glow. I was almost at the cranny when I heard it. The familiar *tap tap tap* of a hammer on rock. A trickle of dust fell out of the tunnel entrance. *Jacob!* Was he back?

I gave a long, low whistle, the secret signal that Jacob had taught me. I held my breath and waited.

Pebbles skittered down to me and dropped on my feet. The whistle was returned, but right away, I knew it wasn't Jacob. Scrambling into the tunnel, I used the handles we'd dug to propel myself up higher. Noah was the only other person besides Romi and me who knew about the tunnel, but he scoffed at it and called the plan foolish.

I whistled again, the sound echoing up the tunnel, to let him know I was on my way. It was met with a reply. Jacob was always reminding me how dangerous a tunnel that went up could be. If Noah slipped, we'd both tumble down. I ducked as dirt and pebbles rained down on me but kept climbing.

"Wondered when you'd decide to join me," Noah said when I hauled myself to below his feet. He looked down, and light from the headlamp shone in my face. His feet were on either side of the tunnel stuck in footholds.

"How many sleeps have you been working?" I asked, miffed that he hadn't asked me to join him. He knew the tunnel mattered to me as much as it did to Jacob.

His rock hammer faltered and he almost lost his grip on it. The system Jacob and I used was that I went first and made a narrow tunnel and Jacob widened it below me. I didn't like being underneath Noah, or the way the rock dust fell in clouds around me. "Only a few. Didn't think he'd be gone this long."

I waited for him to say more. To confirm my fears, that Jacob wasn't coming back. But instead, he surprised me.

"He'll be mad if he sees we haven't been working on it."

"I thought you said it was a waste of time." It was hard to keep the judgment out of my voice. Digging the tunnel after muling all day left me bone tired.

"I want to get out of here as much as you."

"You do?"

He stopped chipping at the rock and looked down at me. "Course, I do. And if Jacob did make it outside somehow, then I know he's waiting for us."

"How come you never helped before?" I asked. "Noah?"

"Wasn't my place," he finally answered. "This was Jacob's way to stay sane. You Unders got your ways. This was his."

"What's yours?" I asked.

Part of me didn't expect him to say anything. As it was, he'd said more to me in the tunnel than ever before. "Who says I have one." I didn't press Noah. He wasn't like Jacob, who I could ask about anything and he'd tell me. When Noah started talking again, it caught me by surprise.

"It's thinking about my people on the Mountain. I've got a daughter, Nadia. She had red hair like mine. Or like it was." He laughed. "Red like hot coals. She'd be grown now. My wife was pregnant when I left, so there'd be another child too."

All my life, Noah was like Old Father. Angry and unpredictable. But hearing his words and how his voice could be soft, made me wonder if I'd been wrong about him.

Sari

I'd barely spoken to Ren as he'd led me out of the Underland. He'd mistaken my silence for sadness and been sympathetic. "It can be hard to see an elder for the last time."

But really, everything Sy had told me was spinning in my head. I needed a quiet place to think. When I got to work, there was another lineup of females waiting for their appointment. My supervisor 'tsked' me. I was two minutes late. No doubt she'd make a note on my file. If Kaia had been here, we would have rolled our eyes at each other. I sat down in my chair and projected the hologram in the air in front of me. Rows of icons filled the screen. One of them, Data Share, blinked at me. It had new content.

My breath quickened. I knew it was from Sy. What had he given me? More nonsensical mumblings? Or was this something that would help?

Outside my cubicle, females were being called for their appointment times. I groaned with frustration. I'd already attracted too much attention from my supervisor. She'd be checking to make sure I stayed on schedule. Anyway, there wasn't enough privacy at work; opening the file was risky because I didn't know what I'd find. I swiped it out of data share into a different folder and tried to push it from my mind.

As soon as my shift was over, I stood up. I ignored the glare from my supervisor. "Low on joules," I said and held up my finger so she could see the number. It was true, I was low and I *should* be going to the gymnasium to earn more, but all I could think about was getting to my dwelling. I wanted to know what Sy had shared with me.

I crossed a bridge over the stream and was halfway to my dwelling when I saw Mika. She'd seen me too, so there was no avoiding her.

Not many birth elders are granted permission to replenish themselves. It was an honour decided upon by the Council. Only those Citizens who had proven that their genetic material would create offspring of the highest standard were chosen to be implanted a second time. Growing up, my sibling Mika had reminded me every chance she got that I owed my existence to her.

Tall and lithe as a stalk of bamboo, she had a grace I did not. She kept her hair short, as was expected, but instead of it looking harsh, her near-baldness was velvety soft, the fair hair shimmery.

"Sari," she said. Mika was four years older and even though I was a full-fledged Citizen and (technically) matched, she still had the ability to make me feel like a child who hadn't had her first Mat Day. She'd always teased me for my relationship with Kaia. Mocking our closeness. I'd throw it back in her face by telling her Kaia was more of sibling than she'd ever be.

"How are you?" A flash of sympathy crossed her face. "I heard about your match," she said. "And then everything else. Any word yet?"

She hadn't sent me any messages—no congratulations for the match, or concern when Lev had been sent out after the missing Citizen. As much as I tried not to let it bother me, it did. I shook my head. "It's been so long," I said. "I'm not hopeful." It was the first time I'd said those words out loud.

Mika frowned. "I'm sorry," she said. There was a long moment of silence. Neither of us knew what to say. "I'm meeting Dex. He should be here any minute if you want to say hello."

After waiting to put her name in, she'd been matched two years ago with a male that made my birth elders beam with pride. At the time, my stomach had twisted with jealousy.

"I should go," I said. "It's been a long day. It was nice to see you."

"You too." As she spoke, I realized there was something different. Months of working at the fetal assessment clinic had taught me the tell-tale signs of early pregnancy: shining eyes, a slight flush to the cheeks, fuller breasts.

"Are you implanted?" I asked suspiciously. It was something to celebrate if she had been and the embryo was viable and growing.

Her smile faded and Mika bristled. I'd ruined her surprise. "Yes. And keep it to yourself."

"Don't worry," I muttered. "I have no one to tell."

She caught my meaning and gave me an apologetic look. Saying 'sorry' had never been one of Mika's strong suits. "It's just—I wanted Dex to be the first to know. After the doctor anyway. I was going to tell him today."

"You've had a lot of good news lately," I said.

"Oh, you heard about my new job?"

Of course, I'd heard. Mika's promotion to Head Geological Engineer had been all over the newsfeed. Mika was the youngest one ever. Her rise had been meteoric. "Yes, I sent you congratulations."

"I had so many. I must have missed it."

It took everything in me not to roll my eyes. "And now you're pregnant. It's wonderful."

She grinned then, smugly.

I tried not to begrudge her happiness. She was my sibling after all. "Will you tell our birth elders?"

"I'm only at eight weeks. I'll send them a message once the implant is at twelve weeks. No need to get their hopes up."

She was right to be cautious. There'd been a lot of problems with new pregnancies lately. We'd been briefed about it at the clinic. "They'll be happy for you." Like always. Mika was a birth elder's dream offspring. A high-status position, the right match, and now, no doubt, a perfect fetus was developing inside of her.

"You're still at the fetal assessment clinic?" she asked.

It was the way she said 'still' that got me. Five letters laced with disdain. "For now," I said.

"Oh?" She pounced. "Reassignment or promotion?"

"It's sort of a special project. For Tar." I regretted the lie as soon as it slipped off my tongue. Well, mostly regretted. The look of sharp, pointed jealousy made the lie worth it.

"What kind of project?"

"Something to do with the Underland. I really can't talk about it."

"What a surprise. You're not the type that usually gets chosen for those sorts of things." I ignored the dig. Mika had finished top of her class. If anyone should have been asked to work on a special project, it was her. "I think of you as so much younger than me, but I guess we're peers in a way now, aren't we? Both of us working our way up in the City hierarchy."

Was that grudging respect? A message must have come through on her communicator because she looked up the walkway and waved.

"He's here," she practically swooned. Dex walked with brisk steps, eager to get to Mika. He was the descendent of a first-generation scientist, one of the creators of the City. Both of his birth elders had held spots on Council. Mika's smile grew bigger as he approached. I wished I could know the person she was with Dex. Instead, I got barbs and insults. Constant reminders that I wasn't good enough; I was only ever an afterthought.

"Send me a message when it's time for your next appointment. I'll make sure you get a good technician at the clinic," I said, but she wasn't listening. Her eyes were on Dex as he came closer.

"Okay. Thanks."

"I hope"—I swallowed back my envy and forced myself to utter the words—"I hope it all goes well."

She gave me a nod of acknowledgement, but all her attention was on Dex. I gave him a quick wave hello and continued on my way.

"Was that Sari?" I heard him ask. Whatever she replied, I didn't hear.

Let them have their moment. Their joy at the new life they'd created with the help of a laboratory and a test tube, I thought bitterly. Another perfect Citizen to live in our perfect City.

The sound of the door shutting behind me echoed in my empty dwelling. As soon as Lev and I had been officially matched, I'd applied for a partner-dwelling. But then he'd left to go after Kaia, and I'd moved in alone. To have all this space to myself was a luxury and I wondered how long it would last. My whole life, the only privacy I'd known had been in my sleeping capsule. Even then Mika had been in the capsule next to mine. I used my pulse point to turn on a few lights. Wasteful considering how few joules I had left, but the brightness helped me feel less alone.

Looking at Sy's file in the middle of the dwelling felt wrong, too exposed. I went into my capsule and sat cross-legged. Then, I took a deep breath and lifted my pulse point. The hologram projected in front of me.

As soon as I swiped to open the file Sy had shared with me, a message popped up. *Permission to view* Mining Access Plan (M.A.P.) *granted.*

I stared in wonder. Sy had said the word map, but what he'd meant was an acronym. M.A.P. Why had he given this to me? The Mining Access Plan was a virtual tour of the Underland. I recognized the start of the tunnels as I flew past the Councillor's chambers and Sy's cell, where I'd visited today. The tour kept going deeper, through a series of corridors and then narrow tunnels until it ended in a huge cave.

I don't know how long I stared at the tunnels and chambers, moving through them until I felt dizzy. My brain was on overload. I tried to remember everything Sy had told me. It wasn't all riddles like I'd thought.

He'd said the truth was buried in the Underland and that the answers were in the pit. I frowned, thinking. Was the pit this hollow space? And what did any of it have to do with 'intertwining'? Or Kaia's disappearance? I rubbed my temples. Trying to make sense of this on my own was giving me more questions than answers.

The beep of my communicator startled me. I rarely got messages now that Kaia was gone. More surprising was that it was from Mika: "It was good to see you today. We should get together sometime. Dinner maybe?"

I sighed and didn't respond. Somehow, having her reach out made me feel even more alone. She wasn't asking because she really cared, she was asking because she felt bad for me, or maybe she'd been urged by Dex. I'd gone from someone on my way up in the City, to someone that needed pity.

Ama

Life in the Underland was hard. Without fathers, the mothers did what they could to keep the children alive, but hunger, darkness and hopelessness plagued them. The children were expected to dig, and *as long as they did, they were fed. Mothers did their best to comfort the children, but madness grew, it spread like a sickness. How could they survive in the depths?*

A mother realized that when she closed her eyes and concentrated, she could escape the cave. She could free her mind. The mother showed her daughter and the two of them would sit on their mats and retreat from the darkness into the light of their minds. The mother imagined Big Mother was speaking to her. The voice said, mah, *so that was what she repeated.*

A peace settled over the mother and her daughter. Others noticed and joined them in their moments of quiet, often using Big Mother's word to block out the noise of the Underland. It lifted their spirits. It bonded them with Big Mother and let them go forward in the dark holding a light in their mind.

So, that is why all us Unders sit together and chant. It's our way of talking to Big Mother and bringing some of her spirit into the darkness.

I'd spent sleep time digging with Noah again and my body was weary and aching. Neither of us had spoken as we'd chipped at the rock. With me and Jacob, it had been different, more peaceful. Sometimes, he'd hum softly under his breath, or tell me stories about the outside, his voice low and soothing. But Noah worked ferociously, as if his life depended on our escape.

We were making progress, but was it enough? Would we break through in time, before Krux found out about Romi's bleeds? And what happened when we got to the surface? I'd always thought Jacob would be there beside me and would know what to do. Would Noah know how to get to the Mountain? Would he take all of us with him?

I folded my legs so I was sitting cross-legged on my mat. We began every shift this way. Romi was on one side and Luken on the other. He pressed his knee tight against mine. I opened one eye a crack to peer at him. His hands were clasped in front of his chest, his spine was straight, his mouth pulled tight with concentration.

I closed my eyes and faced front. The chant, a long, low *mah* began somewhere on the other side. It was a deep voice, so maybe it was Kibo. The sound was a thread that got picked up and added to by each Under it touched. The *mah* echoed off the cave walls and filled the pit. It was our one breath, shared between all of us. Our prayer to Big Mother.

We did three *mahs* three times. The final chord wavered in the air and no one stood up right away. We took our time and soaked up the calm to steady our minds. The dark never felt as deep after we *mah*ed. The *mah* gave us a light that we could carry with us while we worked.

Kibo and Abel were waiting for me at the entrance to the cave tunnels. I felt Kibo looking at me, but I couldn't meet his eyes. "Are you sick?" he asked.

I shook my head. Usually, Jacob and I only worked for a short while so I could sleep. I didn't have that luxury anymore. "Just tired."

"Worried?"

I nodded.

Kibo tweaked my ear. "He'll be back."

I nodded and motioned Luken forward. "Time to put this on," I said. He hung his head but stood still while I tied on the basket as gently as could. He didn't say a word and only winced once. "Guess what? After this shift, we get to soak in the pool."

A timid smile lifted one corner of his mouth. The pool was a gift from Big Mother. She hung near its entrance and I thanked her every time I sank into that warm water. The soreness and chill melted away. Coloured by the salt brine, the cave pool gleamed bright turquoise when light hit it. Lila said the pools were like a *mah* for our aching bodies.

Romi and her team went into the tunnels first. She looked back at me over her shoulder. I held her eyes for as long as I could and then it was time for my team to go in. Kibo figured we had one more day in the hole we were digging. After that, we'd have to move to a different spot. Kibo and Abel would chip through the rock to make a new tunnel. Luken and I would carry the debris away. When they found a spot that looked promising, we'd expand the space.

It was trial and error. There were empty holes all over the Underland that never gave more than a few grains of brine. But other times, one hole could keep a team busy for so many shifts, they'd lose track of how long they'd been in one place.

I stayed at the back of our procession, happy to go slowly with Luken. Every muscle ached. By the time we got to the digging hole, I was already dragging. Kibo raised his eyebrows at me. "You sure you're not sick?"

I knew why Kibo was so worried. Sickness in the pit spread fast. I waved off his concerns and forced myself to give him an energetic nod. "I'm fine." I'd asked Jacob once if we could tell Kibo about the escape tunnel. He'd want to help; I was sure of it. The work would go faster with a strong boy like him, but Jacob had said no. The more people who knew, the bigger the risk.

I showed Luken how to sift through the crumbs on the cave floor for larger chunks. "Every bit matters," I told him. "There's no point leaving any behind. The sooner we get to the quota, the sooner the digging shift is over. I'll stay here and you go look there," I pointed to the middle of the cave. "Don't get under the diggers' feet though," I warned him. "Nothing worse than a mule who's in the way."

The words had just left my lips when a crack split the ceiling. Small at first, it widened as bits of rock and sand fell down on my head. I pressed myself up against the wall; the safest place to be in a cave-in was by a wall. The most dangerous place was under the crack where Old Father could grab you.

"Ama!" Luken's terrified voice filled the cave. I squinted through the rock dust and looked for him. He was frozen in the middle of the chamber, staring up at the growing zigzag crack that had split the ceiling. Old Father's jaw was opening.

Luken's eyes were wide with terror. Chunks of rock fell from the ceiling. A huge boulder shifted and hung over Luken, ready to drop. He needed to move or he was gonna get crushed.

"Luken!" I shouted and lunged, yanking him to my side of the cave just as half the ceiling dropped. Rocks fell to the floor in an explosion of dust that sent all of us coughing.

Deep in the tunnels, I heard other teams shouting to each other, checking that all us Unders were okay. "Must have ripped through a few chambers," Kibo said, waving a hand in front of his face. "We're good!" Kibo shouted back.

I was shaking, racking my brain trying to think of what we'd done to make Old Father mad. I hugged Luken to me. His body stayed stiff. I kneeled to look at him, wiping rock dust off his face. "You're okay," I said, more calmly than I felt. "Next time, get to the wall. It's safer there."

His eyes focused on me as if he'd just noticed I was there. "Next time?" he said. I frowned. *Yes, next time.*

"Old Father has to balance things out. Big Mother gives, but Old Father takes."

A shout came down from a different chamber. I didn't catch all of it, just that someone was hurt. "Who is it?" I asked. I strained to hear when the voice came again.

We waited for the news, but the tunnels stayed silent.

And then: "We need help! She's not breathing!"

I looked at Kibo. "Where's it coming from?"

"That way!" He pointed in the direction Romi's team had gone. My heart thumped. *Please, don't let it be Romi*, I prayed to Big Mother.

"Go check," Kibo said. "I'll stay with Luken."

I didn't stop to think about the possibility of another cave-in. All I wanted to know was that Romi was okay.

Sari

Most evenings after work, I'd cut my running short so I could go back to my dwelling and study the MAP. I'd discovered that I could step through virtual doors and explore narrower tunnels off the main corridor. There were hundreds. A whole world lay under the City that Citizens knew nothing about. Sy had passed the knowledge on for a reason, but I still didn't know what it was.

He said he'd helped her escape, the same way he'd helped Raina, which meant he must have believed Raina had made it. Otherwise, why send Kaia to her doom? I wished he'd told me more. I needed answers and the only person who could provide them was stuck in a cell in the Underland.

"Joule level low," the communicator's voice said in my ear as I left my cubicle at the fetal assessment clinic. "Joule level low." The voice would repeat on auto loop until I went to the gymnasium. With a heavy sigh, I realized I couldn't avoid it any longer. I dragged myself in its direction. I didn't used to mind going when Kaia and I could chat while we ran.

As soon as I stepped on the mat, I wished I'd chosen a different spot. The two females running beside me were too much like Kaia and me: one was blond and the other brunette.

"Unbelievable," the blond one muttered to her friend. I followed her gaze. Two rows ahead, a female elder had stepped onto a mat. Even from where I was, it was obvious that exercise was hard for her. A life of daily running left all Citizens with aching joints. Mae had complained often of her hips and knees hurting. It was why Kaia had energy shared with her: to spare her from having to plod along on a running mat every day. "The Council can't let this go on."

"What are you talking about?" her friend asked.

"Didn't you hear? Because of the culling last month, they ran out of ripe baneberries. All balancings have been suspended. In the meantime, Citizens like her are suffering. It's terrible. The Council shouldn't expect her to earn joules."

"They can't just give out joules."

"Why not? It's short term." She dropped her voice. "I mean, look at her? What if that were your elder?" The brunette nodded. "The worst part is some of them are sitting in cells! I heard that one of the City's original Citizens is down there! Imagine! A First Generation being treated that way! This Council has no respect."

I stumbled and caught myself before I fell. She could only be talking about Mae.

My legs trembled as I stood off to the side. I hadn't run for as long as I intended. My joules hadn't hit triple digits yet, but I didn't care. If that female was right and Mae was still alive, I needed to do something. I'd betrayed Kaia by matching with Lev; I couldn't let Mae die alone, or worse, rot in a cell thinking no one cared.

⌒

"You don't want the orange back, do you? Because I already ate it." Ren grinned at me. He was standing in front of the Underland entrance, still in his overseer uniform.

Despite my nerves, I smiled. "That's not why I asked to see you."

"It was really good," he said, smirking. "You missed out."

"Ren," I said. "This is serious."

The grin disappeared. I looked around to make sure no one was close enough to hear me. "When I went to visit Sy, you said there was another elder being held down there. Do you know if it's a female?"

He nodded.

I got a burst of hopefulness. Was it possible Mae was still alive? "Do you know her name?"

Ren frowned. "It's Mae, I think."

If we hadn't been in public, I would have hugged him. A show of affection in the central square would turn heads. "She's Kaia's second generation elder! We thought she'd been balanced. Please, Ren, can you let me see her?" I'd known Mae my whole life and the news of her balancing had upset me too. In many ways, I was closer to Mae than I was to my own birth elders.

Ren's face hardened all of a sudden. He stood up straighter and clenched his jaw.

I thought I'd offended him, asked for too much, but then I saw that his eyes were trained on someone behind me. "Councillor Tar," he said, nodding as she walked past. She surveyed him with an imperious gaze and her eyes flicked in my direction. She paused. My breath caught in my throat.

"Sari," she said. She gave me a long look. I stared at her chin and clasped my hands together to stop them from trembling. "You still haven't answered my question from our meeting."

I swallowed. Did Tar really see potential in me, or was this a way to keep me close in case I knew more about Kaia's departure than I had let on. My guess was on the latter. I might have taken her up on the offer before, but I was starting to see the City differently. "It's a lot to consider," I stammered.

"Don't take too long. I might find someone else." There was a warning tone in her voice. I doubted Tar was used to being turned down.

Her red robe swished as she strode away.

Ren looked at me puzzled. "What was that all about?" he whispered. We both stood watching as people parted to let her through.

"You wouldn't believe me if I told you," I muttered.

"Listen, if you want to risk it and see Mae, I'll can take you now. It's dinner hour for the overseers. There won't be many in the corridor. But there's a condition."

"What?" I would have agreed to almost anything.

"What did Tar mean about an offer?"

"I'll tell you as we go," I said and nodded for him to lead the way. For the second time, Ren was risking his job for me. I was in his debt.

"Mae?" My voice cracked as I stepped into her cell. Just like Sy's, it was small with a thin mattress against the far wall. Ren was in the corridor. He'd given me only five minutes. I hoped that would be enough. I crouched down and tried to ignore the stench. "It's me, Sari."

Mae stirred and sat up. She squinted into the lightstick's beam. I let out a sigh of relief. Her short grey hair stuck on end and it looked like she was wearing the same tunic she'd had on the day she was taken. To treat Mae, one of the original inhabitants of the City, this way was shocking. She'd done nothing wrong except get old.

"Sari," Mae said. The corners of her mouth moved up in a weak smile. "How did you get in here?" Mae shifted, wincing when a joint cracked. Despite the conditions, her eyes were bright.

"It's a long story. I don't have much time," I said. "Sy helped Kaia escape. She's gone to the Mountain."

"I know," Mae said. "Lev came to see me before he left."

I swallowed. "He did?"

"Yes. He wanted proof before he went after her. I'm an incentive to bring Kaia back. It's a wasted effort. Kaia's not coming back."

"She will if she finds out you're alive."

Mae exhaled slowly. "I hope not. She doesn't belong here anymore."

"What do you mean? Why do you say that?"

Mae pressed her lips together.

"Does her leaving have something to do with intertwining?" I watched her carefully, waiting for a reaction.

Surprise flashed across her face. "Where did you hear that word?"

"It's in her file. Under Sy's name there's an asterisk and then that word. What does it mean?"

Mae took a deep breath. "Sari, you're asking a lot of questions."

"I want to know why she left," I pressed. "All this time, I've been thinking it was because of me and my match with Lev. I want to know the truth."

I thought about the last time I'd seen her. She'd been on her balcony with Lev. When I'd spotted them from the walkway, I'd been relieved. *Kaia's better!* I'd thought. I watched them for a moment, standing shoulder to shoulder. Even from down below, I could see what they meant to each other. Anyone could.

I thought about ignoring them. Let them have their moment together. Kaia would find out about our match soon enough. But watching their closeness, I'd felt a flash of jealousy. Kaia was *my* friend. *I* should be the one up there with her.

"She didn't handle the news about my match with Lev well." I let my voice drift off. Kaia had crumpled on the balcony and

Lev had shooed me away like I was an annoyance. "Do you think that was what pushed her to leave?"

Mae sighed. I steeled myself for her recriminations, but none came. She closed her eyes for a moment. The time in the cell had taken a toll on her. I saw it in the way her shoulders sagged. "Kaia has a secret, and you're right, it has to do with intertwining. Tar knew about it because she was the Councillor who approved the plan. But she would have never let her offspring match with Kaia."

I leaned forward, desperate for Mae to tell me. "Why?"

"Because Kaia is not Sy's offspring. Her birth elder is a Prim named Jacob."

I gaped at Mae. "A Prim? How is that possible? There aren't Prims in the City!"

"Not that you know about," Mae said. I waited for her to explain. "Raina was a thinker, always paying attention to things. She was worried that the City planner's dreams of genetic perfection would be our undoing. No species can survive long term without introducing new DNA. She went to the Council and presented her ideas to them. After living inside the dome for so long, she believed that our bodies would lose the ability to adapt to new environments. The City was only ever meant to be a short-term solution. At some point, we'd have to go back outside.

"Raina thought the answer was to introduce new DNA. It was Tar's idea to capture the Prims. Raina agreed to be implanted with an intertwined child. She thought it would be the first of many, but Tar had other ideas."

Mae paused. I nodded, encouraging her to keep going. "Tar wanted to use the intertwined as a crop. She thought their DNA could be harvested. When Raina figured it out, she was already pregnant with another intertwined. She and Sy decided to leave the City, but at the last moment, Sy got cold feet."

"So all this time, you and Sy kept the truth from Kaia?"

Mae nodded.

"And that's why Tar sent people after Kaia," I realized. "Because she needs to know if the experiment worked."

"Yes," Mae agreed. "And she's made sure I can't warn her." Mae held up her index finger. A grimy bandage, spotted with blood, was wrapped around it. "Or anyone else."

"She took out your pulse point?"

Mae nodded. Her chin trembled. I hated seeing Mae this way. I couldn't imagine what Kaia would do if she found out. "I'm sorry, Mae. You don't deserve this."

Mae gave a rueful laugh and defiance flashed on her face. "Tar's motives are more complicated than you know." Mae gave me a long look. "The City is in danger, especially with Tar running the Council. Whatever you do, don't trust her."

In the corridor outside her room, there was a noise. The bamboo pole slid back. In a second, the door was going to open and our time together would be over. Mae collapsed onto the mattress looking as feeble as when I'd first arrived. Ren peeked his head in. "Ready?" he asked me. I nodded and stood up. He frowned as he looked at Mae. Compassion flashed across his face.

"She shouldn't be in here," I whispered. "She hasn't done anything wrong."

"The Council must have a reason. But I agree, these conditions…" his voice drifted off.

"Goodbye, Mae," I said softly and moved into the corridor. Ren followed and pushed the bamboo pole into place, locking Mae inside. I had no reason to doubt Mae, but what she'd said about Kaia was shocking. How had I not known my best friend was part Prim? Shouldn't there have been some trace of her inferiority? Her primitiveness? It called into question everything I knew about her and everything we were taught about Prims.

"How is she?" Ren asked breaking into my thoughts.

"Stronger than me," I said. "I don't know how she's surviving down here. Thank you for letting me see her." I touched his arm lightly. Ren opened his mouth but before he could say anything an overseer shouted to him from further down the corridor. Ren glanced in his direction. "You should go," he said quietly. "This one's nosey. If anyone stops you, say you were dropping off supplies in storeroom B."

As I made my way towards the stairs that led to the City, there was a sudden vibration. I reached out to the wall to steady myself. It was over in seconds. I looked back for Ren, but he and the other overseer were gone.

Had I imagined the vibration? Had anyone else felt it? I scanned the corridor and noticed a small crack making its way down the wall.

Ama

Long ago, the mothers lived with the children in the Underland, just as they had before they were taken from the outside. They cared for their young ones like Big Mother cared for all the Underlanders. The mothers didn't like seeing their children work. Digging was dangerous, so they refused to send them into the tunnels. The City people got mad. They stopped sending food to teach the mothers a lesson. Still, the mothers kept the children with them.

So, the City people did a horrible thing. The City people tried to take the mothers away. Of course, the mothers fought, refusing to be ripped from their young. But they were punished in the worst way possible. The wails of the children were deafening, they echoed off the Underland walls. They promised to work, to dig more than ever before, but the City people ignored them. The mothers were gone.

But not forgotten. Stories of the mothers and how they'd fought for their children lived on. They were heroes to the Underlander children. The spirit of Big Mother flowed through the mothers and every

new youngun was a gift. A treasure from the mothers, the glorious
creatures filled with light and love who would one day return to their
Underlander children.

The dark tunnel was filled with rock dust. I tucked my chin under
my tunic to avoid breathing it in. Rocks and debris littered the
tunnel and made it hard to crawl through. I gasped when a sharp
rock scraped my leg.

I pulled myself through the narrow opening of the chamber
and searched the space until I found Romi. She was crouched
next to Freya, one of the diggers.

"Romi!" I gasped. I wanted to cry with relief. She was okay.

"I don't know what happened. She was behind me and then..."
she shook her head helplessly. Rubble lay scattered around Freya's
body. "She got caught under the rocks. By the time we lifted
them off, she was gone."

All I could think about as I looked at Freya's body was that
it could have been Romi lying on the ground. "She's safe now," I
said and closed her eyes.

It didn't matter that we'd lost Freya, the quota for brine still
had to reached. So after Romi's team took Freya to Lila, they
went back into the tunnel to dig. Word spread though, and by
the end of the shift, all of us Unders trudged out of the tunnels
with heavy hearts.

We'd keep Freya's body with us until Krux came to take it away.
She was a sacrifice to Old Father and all we could do was hope he was
satisfied. Lila would lead us in the naming when we were all gath-
ered. 'Freya' would be chanted nine times, like a *mah*, so the name
would seep into the walls of the cave and be with us Unders forever.

It hit me that without Jacob, it'd be up to me to mark Freya's
death on the wall.

"I'm sorry about Freya," I said when Romi and I were on our sleeping mat. I'd taken Luken to the pool, but everyone was more subdued than usual. The delicious sensation of water lapping on our bodies was tainted. My eyes strayed over to the cranny. More than ever, I wanted to work on the escape tunnel, dig through the rock and find our way to the surface.

"She was right behind me," Romi said again, shaking her head. "And then the ceiling cracked open. Old Father was angry, Ama. Worse than before." She turned so our noses were pressed together. "Do you think he's angry we're leaving?" Her breath was hot in my face.

"We've been leaving for a long time," I told her.

"You said you're close. What if he doesn't want us to go? What if he's trying to keep us here with him?"

Her words sat heavy on my heart. I'd never considered that. "Big Mother would fight him." I was sure of that. "She wants us to be happy. She'll protect us."

"She didn't protect Freya."

"She can't protect everyone. She has to let Old Father win sometimes." *He can take anyone he wants, as long as he doesn't take you*, I thought and nestled closer to Romi. I wanted to give my warmth to her and soak hers in too. I needed to feel her beside me, every part of our bodies pressed together.

When her breathing got slow and deep, I knew I should leave to dig with Noah, but part of me didn't want to. I just wanted to stay on the mat beside Romi where it was warm and safe and my aching body could rest. So that's what I did. For the first sleep in a long time, I spent all of it on my mat.

When we woke, Noah was at his station doling out food. I went up with my bowl and Romi's. She was still sleeping, and I didn't have the heart to wake her. "I need to talk to you," I said to Noah when I was close enough for him to slop some of the leftovers from last night into my bowl.

"So talk." A line had formed behind me.

"Now?"

"Good as time as any." Noah turned his cheek away from me. "What do we do if the tunnel is ready before Jacob comes back?" I whispered.

He handed the ladle he was using to the next Underlander in line. "Finish up," Noah grunted to him. He grabbed my elbow and pulled me away from the line. "Jacob's not coming back," he said.

"What? What do you mean? How do you know?" Panic rose in my chest.

"Look at your wall! How long's it been?"

"But," I stammered for something to say, a way to argue with him, even though I knew he was right. "Then where is he?"

Noah leaned towards me. "Before we came to the pit, we were prisoners. I think that's where Jacob is."

"What if they, what if he's—"

"Dead? He's too valuable to them."

"What do you mean valuable?"

"It's—you wouldn't understand."

"If he's still alive, we should go look for him."

"Ha! And get caught? Then we'd all be captives. No, I'm going to keep working on the tunnel, which is what I should have done from the beginning." He gave a rueful shake of his head. "The tunnel would be finished by now if I'd helped. The best thing we can do for Jacob is to keep working, to get out of here."

"But if he's being held—"

"You heard me, Ama. He wouldn't want us to risk our lives for him. Not when we're so close to getting out."

I walked away from Noah, numb. I knew he was right about

what Jacob would want, but if it were me being held, or Noah, Jacob wouldn't hesitate. He'd risk everything to find us.

Sari

I t was late at night when I finally put the MAP away and turned off the light in my capsule. I'd been looking for something that would explain the tremor I'd felt that afternoon. I'd come up empty-handed. No matter how many times I explored it, there were always new twists and turns. It was a giant maze. Between all the things Sy, and now Mae, had told me, I knew I was in for another sleepless night. I let out a long sigh. My life had been so much easier before.

As usual, the gymnasium was busy in the mornings before people started their workday. It wasn't my preferred time to be here, but there was someone I knew who ran every morning like the dutiful Citizen she was. My timing was spot-on. Just as I arrived, I saw Mika crossing the square. "Mika!" I called.

She turned and right away, I could see something was wrong. There were dark circles under her eyes. Her face was drawn and tired. "Are you okay?"

"Of course," she said, flashing me a fake smile. "Just excited for my promotion. It's my first day."

I was almost positive it wasn't excitement I was seeing on her face. "Really? So, you're feeling fine otherwise?" I threw a pointed look at her belly.

"I had a few cramps. They kept me up last night."

I gave her a reassuring smile. "It's probably nothing to worry about. Just your body's way of adjusting. If you want to come to the clinic later, I can do a quick scan. Make sure things are okay."

"I didn't say anything about the pain to Dex," she whispered. "I didn't want him to worry."

"It'll be our secret."

Mika bit back a smile. "Thank you."

Mika was about to turn away when I cleared my throat. If anyone could help me learn more about the Underland, it would be her. "Do you like working down there?" I asked, nodding towards the entrance behind her. "You don't miss the light in the City?"

"I've gotten used to it."

"Have you noticed anything different down there?"

"Like what?" she looked at me warily.

There was nothing wrong with what I was about to tell her, but I still hesitated. Could I trust her? Mika peered at me with narrow-eyed interest. "Sari?"

"I was in the Underland yesterday and I felt something. A vibration. It only lasted a few seconds."

A shadow crossed over her face. "Were you alone? Did anyone else feel it?"

Typical Mika. She'd only believe me if someone else could back it up. "No."

"Maybe you just got dizzy and imagined it." She used her best older sibling voice. The one that made me grit my teeth. I opened my mouth to argue, but Mika was having none of it. "I will take you up on your offer for a scan. I'll come by the clinic at noon. Does that work?"

"Yes," I nodded. "I'll be on my lunch break."

"If I were you, I wouldn't mention the vibration to anyone else. It sounds a little"—she searched for the right word—"far-fetched." She'd been a know-it-all before, but now that she was Head of Geology, she'd become impossible.

As Mika walked away, I went into the gymnasium and looked

around for a running mat in the right location. Kaia and I usually waited until we could find two mats together so we could chat while we ran. It wasn't the most efficient way to earn our energy, but we didn't care. I watched a trio of young females giggle and talk nearby. They weren't matching age yet. Part of me wanted to tell them to hang on to these moments as long as they could. I wish I had. I'd been in such a rush to find a mate. Kaia used to tease me about it. She'd sniff the air and ask if it was the scent of ripe compost in the air, or my desperation.

I'd been so foolish. What I wouldn't trade for Kaia to be back in the City.

Ama

For a while, the Underland children lived on their own without the mothers or fathers and hid from the City people. But they needed food and the only way to get it was to send up loads of brine. They prayed to Big Mother to watch over them and protect them. She listened to their prayers and sent nurses, women who never got their bleeds, to raise the new younguns. One of those nurses was Lila, who cared for the rest of them.

Old Father didn't want to be outdone by Big Mother, so he sent them a gift too. He could see they needed guidance, someone to look after them while they dug for brine. He sent two men to watch over them: Noah and Jacob.

But Old Father's mean side had a face too. His name was Krux. Krux with his shifty eyes, pale as the pool, was someone to fear. He carried a zapper that sent jolts that sizzled through your skin and into your blood. The Unders learned quick to obey Krux. Because just like Old Father, he took who he wanted, when he wanted. Sometimes, like with Jacob, he took what back what he'd given.

Another shift was over. Romi and Luken sat on either side of me shovelling food into their mouths. I pushed my bowl of mush away. "Aren't you hungry?" Luken asked.

"You can have it," I said to him. He grabbed it so fast, I would have lost a finger if I'd tried to get it back.

Romi raised an eyebrow, silently asking if I was okay. Her bleeding had stopped as suddenly as it had started. It was going to come back though, and then what? It was only a matter of time till Krux noticed.

"Just thinking," I told her. She didn't ask about what and I was glad. My thoughts were so jumbled up, I couldn't have told her if I'd wanted to. It was her team's turn in the pool, so as soon as she finished eating, she stood up to go.

I looked around the pit. With the big light glowing, I could see the whole space. My 'AMA' marks that covered the walls by our mat and Jacob's tally wall. There was splashing coming from the pool, but mostly, it was the sound of us Unders eating and talking that filled the air. Noah sat at his station by big light and just past him was …what? More Underland, I guessed, although I'd never seen it. The City people were out there and nothing good ever came from them. I imagined them all like Krux, with his watery blue eyes that made me wish I could curl up into a hard shell like a bug.

Lila said Big Mother couldn't protect us once we left the pit, so we stayed where we were. But I wondered if that was true. The mothers were out there somewhere and surely Big Mother was protecting them. Maybe she'd protect me if I went looking for Jacob. If Noah was right, and he was out there, I needed to know.

"Ama!" Luken stomped his foot. He'd licked both bowls clean. I'd been ignoring him, lost in my thoughts.

"What?"

"I want a story," he said.

"Not now," I waved him away. His lower lip quivered.

"But you promised."

I had. It was true. To get him to take an extra load of brine when we were in the tunnels, I'd promised a story and that he could sleep on our mat. "Fine. What story do you want to hear?"

"The one about the first time you saw me. You knew Big Mother had made me the strongest of all the new younguns. You made Jacob promise he'd put me on your team soon as I got big enough to mule."

"You don't need me, you could tell it to yourself," I mumbled. But I started speaking anyway and let Luken crawl right beside me and tuck himself under my arm. Telling the story took my mind off Jacob and where he might be.

"Is that your favourite story, Ama?" Luken asked when I was done.

"I don't know," I said.

"I think it is. I can tell by your voice."

I tweaked his ear, the same way Kibo tweaked mine. "You think you're pretty smart, don't you?"

"Just because we live in the dark doesn't make us dim," he said gravely.

Romi came back to us then, her skin pink and clean from the pool. Big light faded and soon we were in the dark again. "You staying here?" she asked Luken as she lowered herself to the mat, feeling for her spot beside me.

"Ama said yes."

I was glad it was dark because I didn't have to see the eye roll Romi would have given me. "Softie," she whispered.

I waited until the sounds of sleep filled the pit before I carefully slid off the mat. Luken murmured in his sleep and shifted closer to Romi, seeking her warmth. Noah would be digging, and I knew I should join him. But I kept thinking about Jacob and where he might be. If I was ever going to look for him, this was the time to do it.

Big Mother, what should I do? I held my breath, waiting for her to give me a sign.

"You going?" Romi whispered, half asleep.

I rolled off the mat. Guess that was as good a sign as any.

"Yeah. I'll be back soon."

"Hmph," came Romi's muffled reply. I tiptoed, careful not to disturb anyone on their mats. I hesitated and asked Big Mother to watch over me. Instead of going towards the pool, I headed for Noah's station and grabbed a headlamp.

The first step I took past where he sat made my heart beat harder in my chest. I waited for something to happen. For Old Father to swallow me up, or for him to shake the cave in anger. But it stayed silent. Just the snores of the Underlanders behind me. I took a few more steps and put the headlamp on. The walls lit up and I could see the passage ahead of me. I took a deep breath. Krux's smell was everywhere. My stomach turned the way it always did at the smell of him.

The passage was taller and wider than our digging tunnels; I could stand up in it. Not far from the entrance, the passage split two ways. I stood at the fork and put my nose to the ground. Mixed in with the odour of dirt and dampness, I caught it, faint, but familiar. Jacob's scent.

I aimed the headlamp down the passage so I could see what was up ahead and started walking. There were doors carved into the corridor walls. Pressing myself against the wall, I inched forward and nudged open the first door. The room was dark, but Krux's sharp, nose-stinging smell lingered in the air. I looked around. A table sat in the middle, but other than that the room was empty. Backing out, I let the door close behind me. Doors stretched down the passage and I wondered if there were even more around the corner.

The next few I opened held nothing but sleeping mats, and one was completely empty. In another were piles of tunics. I turned a corner and as soon as I did, caught a whiff of something. It was a human smell, strong and fetid. Underlanders? Was Jacob in there?

Unlike the other doors, this one had a bar across it. *Of course, doors that I could easily open wouldn't have anything worth protecting.* The bar was a heavy, but years of muling had made me strong. I used my shoulder for leverage, slid it back and pushed the door open.

Sari

Mika showed up at noon on the dot. Her punctuality was a source of pride for her; I found it irritating. She came into one of the examination rooms and lay down on the table. I hiked up her tunic. When she was lying down, her belly barely showed the pregnancy. When the scanner touched her bare skin, little bumps dotted her flesh. "Sorry," I apologized. "It's cold."

She gave me a nervous smile. I turned the screen so she could see. "There's the head and the spinal cord." I pointed out the sac her fetus was swimming in. "Everything looks fine," I said. "It's developing normally."

Mika gave a long sigh of relief.

I let Mika stare at the blurry image on the screen for a few minutes and then flicked off the machine. Mika pulled her tunic down and sat up. "This morning, when you asked me about the tremor," she started. "I'm sorry I was short with you. I couldn't talk about it in the open."

I'd started to wrap up the cord on the scanner and I paused. "So there is something going on in the Underland?"

Mika didn't answer right away, which made me more curious. "The Underland is different than what people think. It's not just Councillor's chambers and a few workstations. There's a whole world down there. The tunnels go on for kilometres. Some of them aren't even mapped. They're old too, left over from Before."

I pushed the scanner out of the way, busying myself and trying not to look too interested. After studying the MAP for hours, I knew more about the Underland than Mika could have guessed. "Why were the tunnels built?"

"A long time ago this whole valley was covered with a prehistoric ocean. When the ocean dried up, it left behind salt deposits on the ground. Salt, when it's converted, can be an energy source. The tunnels were dug to mine the salt. But when the City was built, they didn't need to dig anymore because we could produce our own energy on the mats. The tunnels are still down there. Abandoned, supposedly.

"Supposedly?" I asked. "Why do you say that?"

"The tremors are getting more common. I've felt them and so have other people. The Geology Department has sensors that monitor changes in the rock density. From what I've seen, it's changing. The only explanation is that either there's an underground fault line that went unnoticed by the original designers of the City, or—"

"—the tunnels are growing," I finished. Mae's warning about the City being in danger echoed in my head. Is this what she meant? "Have you told anyone?"

"Whenever we bring up our concerns, the Council brushes them aside. The Head Geologist before me was also studying the changes. When he went before the Council, not only did they ignore him, they demoted to him to the sanitation department and promoted me. I'm on strict orders not to investigate the tremors. There's something down there the Council doesn't want me to find."

I collapsed onto a chair, as shocked that Mika was taking me into her confidence as about her revelations. "Now that you know all this, what are you going to do?" I asked.

"I don't know." I'd never heard her sound so listless. "Dealing with the Council is frustrating. They don't take me seriously. I think," Mika paused, frowning. "I think I got the job because I'm young and they thought I could be controlled."

I gave a soft snort of laughter. "They don't know you very well, do they?"

Mika smiled and her mood shifted. She pulled up her pulse point hologram, swiped through some messages and sighed. "I have to get back to work." As she stood up from the table, she looked at me. "I was serious about my invitation to join Dex and me for a meal. Come tonight. We eat at the kitchen by our dwelling."

This time, the invitation didn't make me feel pitied. "I'd love to. I'll come by after work."

"It goes without saying that everything I've said—"

"Won't leave this room. I promise." I put my hand up, a gesture from Before that meant a promise.

"Thanks. And thanks for this," she pointed to the scanner. "At least I'm not stressed about one thing in my life."

After Mika left, I wished I could have sent Kaia a message. Not just about what I'd learned about the Underland, but also to tell her Mika and I had spent fifteen minutes in the same room and neither of us had run away screaming. Missing Kaia had become a familiar ache, but every so often, like now, the pain was knife sharp.

⌒

Dex and Mika were at the communal kitchen, just as they said they'd be. But they weren't alone. When I saw who was with them, I stopped dead in my tracks.

Ren had changed out of his overseer tunic into a plain one. "Glad you could make it," he said when I got to the table. "Surprised?"

"Confused," I said slowly. He grinned at me and slid over on the bench so I could sit. A bowl and cutlery had been laid out for me. Another person was there too, a male I didn't recognize. "This is Avi. He's an engineer," Mika said.

Avi nodded in greeting.

Dex went about ladling out soup into each bowl. There was lentil bread as well, the kind our birth elder used to buy at the market.

"Mika says you work for the Council," Avi began.

"Sort of," I hedged and looked at Ren, waiting to see if he corrected Avi. He'd heard Tar ask me about it and afterwards I'd explained my misgivings. *Working for* had been an exaggeration meant to impress Mika.

"Can you be specific?" His question came out like an interrogation.

"Avi, relax. You're going to scare her away," Ren laughed. But the way Dex and Mika leaned in, I could tell they were curious too.

How much could I tell them? After our conversation this afternoon, I trusted Mika, but I didn't know Avi at all. I shot a questioning look at Mika. She nodded.

"It's okay," Ren prompted. "We're all here for the same reason."

"Which is what exactly?" I looked at Mika. I thought she'd invited me to be nice, but it was becoming apparent that our sibling bond had nothing to do with it. Mika fixed me with one of her steely glares. It used to be reserved for the times I begged her to energy share because I'd dilly-dallied instead of going to the gymnasium. But this time, the look felt so much heavier. "Welcome to the CORE," she said. "That's what we call ourselves. It's an acronym for collect, organize, reveal, and explain."

I saw now why she'd cast a furtive look around the kitchen. "Collect, organize, reveal and explain what?" I asked.

"The truth about how the City is really run. Right now, just watch and ask questions. We're curious about a lot of things, especially what goes on in the Underland." Ren and Mika worked down there. Dex's job as a communication specialist was housed across the stream from most of the dwellings, close to the fetal assessment clinic. And Avi? Did he work in the Underland too?

Ren started speaking in a low, intense voice. "There's a lot about the City that doesn't add up. We're trying to make sense of what we know—"

"And don't know," Mika interrupted.

"About the City," Ren finished.

"The Council too," Dex added.

"Basically, everything we're told not to question." Ren met my eyes. "After running into you again, I suggested we invite you. I had no idea you were related to Mika."

I thought back to our conversation. I hadn't hidden my disgust for the way Sy and Mae were being treated, and neither had he. "It was your idea?" I asked.

He nodded. For the first time since Kaia had disappeared, my spirits lifted. I'd felt so alone these last few weeks. "How long have you been working together?"

"A few months, right Avi?"

He nodded. "I'm part of the engineering team that tracks energy consumption and production."

I gave a silent groan. Citizens made lots of jokes about the type of person who went into energy tracking. Small-minded joule counters who liked nothing better than catching people on energy fraud.

"I did an audit, sort of a personal project, and noticed things weren't adding up. There was no way the Citizens were producing enough energy to sustain us."

I held up my pulse point. Thirty-five glowed through my finger. "Energy in, equals energy out." The City's mantra had been drilled into my head since before my first mat day.

All of them shook their heads. "No," Ren said. "That's what the Council wants you to believe. We think it's more complicated than that."

Avi dropped his voice and picked up where Ren left off. "Running gives everyone a purpose. Sure, the sustainability piece of it is important, the Scientists were right about that, but there's no way the energy produced on running mats could power a City, especially one this big. There has to be an alternate energy source."

"There's the lightning rods and the wind turbines," I pointed out. "They produce energy too."

"Not as much as you'd think," Avi said.

"We think the energy is coming from the tunnels," Mika whispered. "We think they're growing because salt is being mined down there."

"But mining's not a job," I said.

Dex took a sip of his soup. I'd forgotten a bowl was even in front of me. "Not for Citizens maybe, but someone's down there digging."

"Between the tremors, the changes in bedrock density and the Council's refusal to consider it an issue, something is going on. I've secretly run tests on the Underland rock and found traces of salt deposits. I've done my research. I *know* I'm right. If I were allowed to explore further, I bet I'd find a vein of it. And who knows what else." Mika raised an eyebrow and looked around the table.

"I did some research too," Dex said. "The communication department has access to City records, all the way back to when the City was being constructed. There's mention of diggers, the people who mined for salt in the Underland. The records talk about a pit that was dug, a big open area where the miners congregated. You'd think that would show up on a map of the Underland. But it doesn't. Not even on the maps that Mika uses for work. The last information I could find on the diggers was something about an uprising and that's it. It's like they just disappeared."

"But the tunnels are expanding," I said, putting the pieces together. "So someone's down there digging."

Mika nodded. "We want to know who and why."

Mika had never been the type of person to push boundaries. She was the dutiful firstborn; the one so perfect our birth elders were granted permission to produce again. But she was serious about solving this mystery. "See over there," she turned her head towards a section of the dome. "The ground is weakest there. If the dome were to collapse in that section, the whole thing would come crashing down. All the panels are connected."

"Without a dome, we'd be at the mercy of the climate. And we all know how that worked out," Avi raised an eyebrow. My stomach turned at the thought of living outside. It was a death sentence. All of a sudden, the intertwining project made more sense.

Mika looked at me and then gave a pointed look to her belly. She had more than just herself to think about now. "The Council knows more than they're admitting, but not doing anything is only making the situation worse."

"There's no doubt, the Council is keeping things from us." Avi's voice was sour.

"The Council? Or Tar?" Ren had a steely look in his eye. "She's at the root of all of this. She dangles incentives in front of people, keeping them close. I don't trust her."

I let everything they'd said sink in. It was a lot to consider.

I thought about the MAP and how it might give them some answers, especially Mika. "What do you want from me?" I asked.

This time, Ren spoke. "We need information."

"Like what?"

"We want you to go back to Mae and find out more about what she remembers from the City's beginning. She's the last of the original inhabitants. Maybe she knows something about diggers and what happened to them."

I thought carefully before I said, "She might have already given me something helpful. Well, it came from Sy, actually. But it was Mae's to begin with. Her birth elder was one of the City's designers." They looked at me expectantly. No one made a sound as I explained. "It's a 3D map of the Underland but it's called a Mining Access Plan."

"Why did Sy give this to you?" Dex asked.

The warning not to trust people echoed in my head. But they had as much to lose as I did. I looked around the table and decided it was worth the risk. Mae had told me the City was in danger, and now Mika had confirmed it. Doing nothing was no longer an option. "I wanted to know why Kaia left. He said it would help explain things."

"Where is it now?" Avi asked.

"On my pulse point," I replied. He frowned, and his eyes darted over my face like he was assessing me.

"It might not be accurate," Mika said.

Avi shook his head. "The maps the Council approves are the ones we have to worry about. They remove the things they don't want you to know about. If Kaia's MAP came from one of the original inhabitants, it hasn't been altered. We could find out what the Underland *really* looks like."

"I've spent hours studying it. At the end of one of the tunnels is a space that sounds like the pit Dex read about."

"We still need to verify it. There's no point using a MAP from decades ago that's incorrect," Mika said. "Someone has to go into the Underland and see if what Sy gave to Sari is authentic. If it isn't, we're just wasting our time."

Dex nodded. "I could arrange it. I've scrambled pulse points before."

I looked at Dex, startled. "You have?" A scrambled pulse point meant you were undetectable to the City. Only a communication technician would have access to the technology and the know-how to do it.

He winked at Mika. "Not often, but it was for a good reason."

Mika shot him an irritated 'Now's the not the time' look. Scrambling a pulse point was an extreme way to find privacy, but I had no doubt lots of pre-matched couples did it. They just needed to know the right technician to pay off with joules. "It's too dangerous for one person. If you got caught, we won't be able to help you."

"So two people getting caught is better?" I asked. She and Dex had more on the line than any of us now that Mika was pregnant. "Sy gave me the MAP. I should go."

Mika frowned at me. "Not alone," she said shaking her head.

"I'll go with her," Ren said.

"It's decided then." I locked eyes with Mika. I wasn't entirely sure what I'd gotten myself into, but there was no turning back now. One thing was for sure, there was a lot more to the Underland than Councillors' chambers and storage rooms.

Our privacy didn't last. Three people sat down at the end of the table. The five of us ate our cold soup and lentil bread in silence. Avi rose first and thanked Dex and Mika for the meal. "He lives in the singles complex," Ren said as he walked away. "By choice."

I stared at his departing back. The complex was for unmatched adults. Some were waiting to be matched, and others had been matched and their mate had died. Very few Citizens chose not to be matched. "Why?" It was lonely living without a mate. Why would anyone choose to live that way?

"He says his morals won't let him."

"Morals? What do they have to do with anything?" Creating offspring and growing old with a mate was an important part of being a Citizen. We were expected to replenish ourselves. It was our duty.

Ren leaned in close. His breath was warm against my ear. "He's a little odd. Keep your distance from him."

Dex let his spoon rest in the empty soup bowl. He gave a slight nod towards the walkway that ran parallel to the stream. I pretended to stretch and looked over my shoulder. The five Councillors marched past. They weren't hard to spot in their scarlet robes. Most people paused their conversations to watch them. Our newsfeeds kept Citizens apprised of their actions and the decisions they made to ensure our safety. But only Councillors were allowed in the meetings. I shrank back, relieved that Tar hadn't noticed me. The Councillor walking beside her was Ren's birth elder.

"I never realized how much you look like him," Dex said to Ren, nodding at the Councillor.

"Appearance is the only similarity between us." Ren scowled at the five of them. He didn't realize how lucky he was to be the offspring of a Councillor. His life as a Citizen with status guaranteed him a good job and a desirable match. Mika had done well with Dex, but her match had more to do with her promise as a geologist than with the status of our elders.

"I heard that Councillor Brar is looking for candidates. He's planning on stepping down," Dex said. "Maybe your elder will suggest you."

Ren snorted. "Doubt it." What had started as a democracy had morphed over the years. Now, the five Councillors replaced themselves with a suitable candidate that was agreed to by the other Councillors. "Brar's been grooming his offspring since birth."

"It shouldn't be like that," Mika said. "We should go back to everyone getting a vote."

Dex nodded. "Some people think it caused too much upheaval, all the voting and campaigning, but look what we have now. The Council runs the City. They do whatever they want and there's no one to stand up to them."

"There's us," I said.

"Yeah, well five people having a discussion over dinner might not lead to any real change." Dex sighed.

"It's a start," Mika said.

"Always the optimist." Dex rubbed her shoulder and smiled.

I found myself alone with Ren after Dex and Mika left for their dwelling. "It's a nice night for a stroll," Ren said. A joke amongst City people: it was always a nice night for a stroll in a climate-controlled dome. "Or is that not allowed since you're matched?"

"I'll make an exception this once," I said standing up. We went to the wash station and sanitized our bowls and utensils.

Strolling had been a favourite pastime for Kaia and me. We liked walking along the meandering stream as evening fell in the City. Outside, it was dark, but inside was warm and safe and glowed with light. Other couples, some with their children, walked together or sat on benches. Ren kept a slow pace and neither of us said anything for a while. It was comforting to have his company, for lots of reasons.

We stopped at a bridge and leaned over, looking at the stream below. "Kaia and I used to stroll," I told him. "Sometimes Mae would come with us."

Upstream, two young Citizens dropped bamboo boats in the water. Just like Kaia and I used to do. For a minute, both boats floated, then they shot downstream towards us as the current picked them up. One female stayed where she was, watching hers intently. The other one raced alongside, giggling. At this moment, in the lamplight, the City felt peaceful. Citizens were content, strolling and enjoying themselves. "I can't imagine leaving," I murmured.

"Why do you think Kaia left?" Ren asked.

The guilt of my match with Lev, which was never far away, came rushing back at me. I sighed under its weight. "I used to think it was my fault." I explained about the match and Tar's manipulation. "As hurt as she was, I just don't know if it would have pushed her to leave. The more I learn about Kaia, the more I wonder if there was something else going on."

"Like what?"

I hesitated. I knew Mae had told me to be careful who I trusted. But Ren had risked his job to let me visit with Sy and Mae. He was part of the CORE and had shown his disdain for the Council more than once. If there was anyone I could confide in, it was Ren. "Mae told me Kaia was part of an experiment called intertwining." The words sat heavily in my mouth. I leaned closer to Ren. "She's part Prim."

Ren's eyes widened with surprise. "Part Prim?" he muttered. "How?"

"Mae said her birth elder was the leader of the experiment."

"Where'd the Prim DNA come from?"

"That's the weirdest part. Mae said there were Prims in the City. In the Underland."

"Do you believe her?"

"I have no reason not to."

"Wow." Ren shook his head. "Did Kaia know? Is that why she left? Was she ashamed?"

I shrugged. It hadn't occurred to me that she might be embarrassed about who she was. I would have hidden it, kept it a secret as long as I could, forever if possible—or until it was time for me to be matched. Bit by bit, I was understanding how hard it would have been for Kaia to keep her secret if she'd stayed in the City.

"I guess it could explain why she wanted to leave." He stared at the water for a moment. "You said Kaia knew she and Lev had no chance of being matched, but outside—"

His thinking dawned on me. "They can be together," I finished. I'd assumed Kaia had left first and Lev had been sent by Tar to bring her back. But what if that was what they wanted it to look like? What if Lev had been in on Kaia's plan the whole time? What if when he'd left, he'd never planned on returning?

Ama

It wasn't Jacob behind the door. Instead, five women lay on sleeping mats pushed together so they covered the floor. They wore dirty tunics, the same as we wore in the pit. The air was warm and damp, filled with their odour. I gobbled up every piece of them with my eyes. One had a round belly, just like Big Mother. Only these women were nothing like Big Mother. Big Mother glistened. She gave us new life, all pink and fresh. These women were filthy and stinking. How could they be the mothers?

One was awake. She nudged another with her foot. "Who are you?" she asked. One by one, they woke up, blinking in the light of my headlamp, sleepy and confused.

"I'm Ama," I said.

One of the mothers bolted upright when I said my name. "Ama?"

"Sela!" My voice caught in my throat. She'd been a digger on Romi's team till her bleeds had started. It hadn't been so long ago. I remembered Jacob putting the mark on the wall when Krux took her away. I also remembered her sobbing so hard Krux gave her a zap to quiet her. I had held Romi close that night praying

to Big Mother that that would never happen to her. Or that I'd
have the strength to stop Krux if it did.

Sela stepped over the other mothers, who didn't move from
their mats. "Why are you here?"

I opened my mouth to explain, but the words wouldn't come.
It didn't make sense that this was where the mothers lived. How
could they grow those fresh, pink younguns in this? "I'm looking
for Jacob," I finally spit out.

"Jacob?" Sela asked.

"He was taken by Krux. I thought maybe he was trapped
somewhere."

All the mothers were wide awake now. One had a tunic
stretched tight across her belly. Another had dingy skin and
hair that hung in clumps. Sela was the youngest, but I recognized
the mother beside her. Valla had been a mule too. "Why'd he get
taken?" she asked.

"We don't know."

"Noah's still there?" the one with the big stomach asked.

I nodded. "Krux only took Jacob." I looked around the room.
"You're all mothers and this is where you live?" I asked, still not
believing it.

"Thought it'd be different, huh?" The one with the dingy
skin frowned when she said it.

"What do you do? Just sit around?"

"We have to rest to grow the babies," Sela said. "But we're
useful. Even if we aren't digging or muling. Olga's been here the
longest. She teaches us things. How to care for the babies and
look after ourselves so we can grow them strong."

"We sew all the tunics for the City people. Other things too,"
Olga said. I wondered how many of the younguns had come from
her. "Zila braids baskets when we get straw." She nodded to the
one with the dingy skin.

Would Romi be happy here? Working alongside them? It was calm and quiet. She wouldn't have to mule. Her life wouldn't be in danger every time she stepped into the tunnels, but being a mother was nothing like we had imagined.

"Where's the fathers?" I asked. "Jacob said you need fathers same as mothers to make the babies."

All the mothers looked at each other, but it was the oldest one who spoke. "We've never seen the fathers."

"But Krux takes the boys somewhere," I said, confused. "Where do they go?"

The mothers shrugged. "It's not fathers that make the youn-guns. It's all the test tubes in Krux's lab."

Olga lay back down, punching her mattress to flatten it out. "I need to sleep," she said.

Valla frowned. "You should be careful. We never know when Krux is going to check on us. You'll get in trouble if he finds you here."

"Don't listen to Valla," Sela said, reaching for me. "You can stay. Visit with us. Have you seen my youngun?"

I looked at Sela. "You had a youngun?"

Her eyes glistened. "A boy. Olga said not to name him, but I did." She got a gooey look on her face. "It's Caleb."

"We haven't had a youngun in a while. The last one was a girl."

"That can't be right," Sela looked at the mothers, confused. "Where is he then?"

Olga sighed and rolled over. "Krux kept him."

"What for?" Sela's voice was high-pitched and strangled.

A cold knot lodged itself in my belly. I didn't want to know the answer.

"He just does. It's all you need to know. That goes for all of you. The less we know the better. We grow babies and that's it." Zila's voice was angry when she spoke.

Sela squeezed her eyes shut and wrapped her arms around herself like she was breaking apart. And maybe she was. Knowing a youngun was going to the pit where it'd be raised in a nest with other younguns and nurses was one thing. To think her baby had ended up with Krux was something else. "You all knew this might happen and never told me." It was an accusation.

"We couldn't. Not for your first," Olga said.

"You'd have figured it out eventually. The ones he's gonna send to the nest he lets us keep longer to get them plump and strong. The other ones, he takes right away."

"Like Caleb," Sela murmured.

"You should go," Valla said again.

"He's probably dead," Olga said from her mattress.

"Who?" I asked.

"Jacob. Krux probably killed him."

I shut my ears to her words. She was more like Old Father than Big Mother. "Don't say that," Sela said. "Let her keep hoping. Hope's all she's got."

Sometimes when Luken fell asleep on my mat, he'd kick out in his sleep and catch me in the stomach. Hearing the way the mothers talked and seeing where they lived made me feel the same way. Like I wanted to puke and cry at the same time.

"I'm going," I said to them.

"Are you coming back?" Sela asked.

"I'll try," I said and then slipped back into the tunnel and looked both ways to make sure Krux wasn't lurking in the shadows. When I knew it was safe, I shut the door quietly and put the bar back into place. Part of me wished I'd never opened that door. I needed to get back to the pit. But all the corridors looked the same. For the first time in my life, I was lost. I took a big sniff of the air trying to pick up any trace of the pit. Nothing. I went on my hands and knees. The rocky ground wasn't worn smooth by all us Unders. It had sharp bits of gravel that dug into my skin. No matter which way I turned, I couldn't find a scent that would lead me back.

Please Big Mother, help me! What would Krux do if he found me? Panic rose in my throat, thick like sludge. This was Old Father punishing me for leaving the pit.

I'd been foolish and now I was paying for it.

I'm sorry, Old Father. Don't be mad. I'll go back to the pit and I'll never leave again. If you want Jacob, you can have him. I understand. We got him for all these years, and now he's yours. But please, help me get back to Romi. I was thinking so hard on Old Father that by the time I realized there were other voices in the tunnel, it was too late. There was nowhere to hide and nowhere to run because I didn't know which way was safe. I took off my headlamp and held it in my hands.

Please, Old Father.

Please.

Sari

When I woke up in the morning, I had a message from Ren asking if I was okay, which made my cheeks flush. I'd left him on the bridge, claiming a stomachache, but really, I just needed to be alone with my thoughts. Wondering if Lev and Kaia had planned their escape together had kept me up late last night. I'd gone from the betrayer to the betrayed.

I stretched, letting my body wake up, and heard a knock on my door. It was early for a visitor, which is why I immediately got worried. Had my visits to Mae and Sy been discovered? Was an overseer at my door? I gulped, but didn't have a choice not to answer. Overseers could barge in if they wanted. A Citizen's privacy wasn't worth compromising the City's safety.

I stood on my side of the door and pressed my cheek against it. "Who is it?"

"It's me."

I let out a sigh of relief at Mika's voice.

"I brought the vegetables we talked about." When I opened the door, she was standing with a basket of produce. "This is all extra," she said. She lifted up a tomato and underneath I saw the familiar fabric of an overseer uniform.

"Thanks," I said and took the basket from her. "Do you want to come in?" Dwellings were small, and it wasn't usual to invite people in, but a sibling delivering produce wouldn't raise any eyebrows. I had no doubt my neighbours wondered how a single female had been able to keep a couple's dwelling for so long.

"I can't stay long. I'm expected at work," Mika said loudly from the landing. But as soon as the door was shut, she put down the basket and pulled out the tunic. "Ren smuggled one of his uniforms to me last night. I stayed up late tailoring it for you. It's not going to be perfect, but at least you can slip into the Underland unnoticed."

This was really happening.

"Ren will be waiting at the entrance in ten minutes. We thought it would be better to go early, before the day shift begins. Dex is tracking both of you and will scramble your pulse points as soon as you leave your dwelling. You'll be offline, so we won't know where you are. But neither will anyone else."

I nodded. Mika bit her lip and furrowed her brow. "Are you angry I pulled you into this?"

I gave her a long look. "No. I want to do this."

"I don't think I could go," she confessed. "I had no idea," she broke off. "I don't mean this as an insult, but I didn't know you were so brave."

Her words caught me by surprise. They might have been the

first compliment she'd ever given me. "You better go. It won't look good if the supervisor is late on her first week on the job."

"Be safe, okay?"

"I will."

When Mika left, I shut the door and inspected the uniform. It had a high neck and hung longer than a regular tunic. Though not as flowing as a Councillor's robes, overseer's uniforms had an air of formality about them that set them apart from Citizens' clothing. As soon as I put the uniform on, I felt different. I'd spent my whole life being either afraid or impressed by overseers and now I found out all that made them different was their outfit.

I grabbed a lightstick and unlocked the door. The walkway was quiet. At first, I kept my head down, but then I remembered how overseers walked: head up, shoulders back. I'd draw more attention to myself if I looked meek.

I scanned the square in front of the gymnasium for Ren. He was standing in front of the stream. He raised one eyebrow when he saw me and made his way over. "Feeling better?" Ren asked.

I nodded; I didn't trust myself to speak. Nerves had wreaked havoc with my stomach on the walk over. Having Ren beside me helped. He moved in front of me and down the stairs. As an overseer, he went down there every day and didn't think twice about it. But sneaking me in to explore parts unknown put both of us in danger. I hesitated at the top. We didn't know what we were getting into.

Was finding out the truth about the City's secrets worth the risk?

I wished Kaia were here. She was the one who took charge; she'd know what to do. I looked down the stairs and gripped the lightstick tighter. Mae trusted me. She'd told me secrets about Kaia. Sy must have too, because he'd given me the MAP. For the first time in my life, someone had seen my potential. I couldn't let them down.

I set my foot on the first stair and knew there was no going back.

⌒

The further we went in the Underland, the staler the air became. A few other overseers passed us and both times Ren nodded in greeting. I did the same. But the further we got from the surface, the fewer people we saw. The corridor changed from carefully carved, smooth walls with ceiling cut-outs to narrow, crudely dug and uneven passageways. Ren had to duck so his head wouldn't hit the ceiling.

"Can you check the MAP?" Ren asked when we reached a fork in the tunnel.

I'd planned our route before I'd left my dwelling, memorizing every turn, but actually being in the tunnels was a lot different than flying through them on my hologram.

As soon as it appeared in the air in front of us, the MAP zoomed in on our exact location. "I'm pretty sure the tunnel to the left is a dead end."

"So we go right," Ren said.

I nodded and by manipulating the MAP, navigated our path deep into the Underland until the same dark hole I'd stared into before loomed in front of us. "That's it," Ren breathed. "The pit." Somewhere behind us, there were voices. I curled my finger and the hologram disappeared. Ren and I started off at a faster pace.

The corridor went downhill and shrank. We both had to walk bent over to avoid scraping our heads on the ceiling. "Nervous?" Ren asked. "I saw your finger trembling when you pulled up your hologram."

"Aren't you?" I asked.

"Of course," he answered quickly. "But I'm used to the Underland. I was surprised you volunteered. It's risky."

The truth was, I'd lain awake last night coming up with reasons to back out. In the end, I'd decided I'd already lost what mattered to me. Kaia was gone and the match I'd been so desperate to secure had been a failure. But Mae, Mika and the rest of the CORE were counting on me. I couldn't let them down.

I opened my mouth to try and answer his question, but Ren stopped short and turned to me with his finger to his lips. He gestured for me to pull out the MAP. I did and when it zoomed in on our location, I saw what had drawn Ren's attention. The door across the tunnel wasn't on the hologram. A sliver of light shone under it. We were deep in the Underland now. Why would there be a room so far away from the entrance? Who was inside of it?

I looked at him. "What do we do?" I whispered as I closed the MAP.

He led me to a nearby tunnel. It was even more narrow than the corridor we'd been in. Ren pulled his taser out of its holster and tucked his lightstick away. I did the same and we were plunged into darkness. "We wait," Ren whispered. We stayed huddled against the wall. I was sure whoever was inside the room could hear my heart hammering in my chest.

Behind the door, there was a shuffle of feet, the quiet hum of a lightstick turning on and then the door opened. A lock slid into place. Whoever had left the room didn't want anyone else going inside. I opened my eyes as the person walked past us. His lightstick illuminated his face just enough that I could see who it was. My breath caught in my throat.

Ren and I waited, pressed against the wall, until he'd turned a corner. "Did you see who that was?" he whispered to me.

I nodded. "Krux."

"This must be his lab." Ren moved closer to the door,

inspecting the lock. It was the kind that connected to a pulse point. Only Krux could open it. He'd be alerted if anyone else tried.

"Maybe we should go back," I said.

Ren shook his head. "We've come this far. Anyway, he's gone for now."

"What if comes back?" My stomach sank at the thought of being discovered by Krux. Suddenly, the risk had begun to outweigh the reward. But Ren was already moving further down the corridor and I had no choice but to keep up with him.

"Ren," I whispered. I pulled on his arm to get him to stop. "Did you hear that?"

He stopped and listened, but we were met with silence. Ren turned to me and raised his eyebrows, asking if we could keep going. I nodded and lifted my lightstick so it lit up as much of the tunnel as possible.

Its beam landed on a tiny, filthy creature. She crouched against the wall with her arm covering her face. I looked at Ren. He was staring at her in shock. "It's okay," I breathed, more to myself than to her.

I took a step forward, but Ren put a hand on my arm, stopping me from going closer. The female stayed hunched over but lifted her face and peeked out at me with enormous eyes. Her hair grew in patchy tufts all over her head. Every bony joint was visible on stick-thin arms and legs. The tunic she wore barely covered her.

"She's just a child," I said to Ren and pulled my arm out of his grip so I could crouch down.

I held up my hands to show her I meant no harm. She lowered the arm blocking her face. She was still wary of me. I saw her eyes dart between me and Ren. "Who are you?" I said slowly. "What's your name?"

"Ama." Her voice was only a whisper.

"Are you hurt?" she shook her head, but her eyes didn't leave my face.

I looked at her finger. There was no pulse point, nothing to identify her as a Citizen. "Do you live down here?" I asked.

She nodded.

I turned to Ren. He was staring at Ama, dumbfounded. "Ama, we live in the City. Do you know the City?"

Again, she nodded. "We dig brine for you," she said.

Mika had been right about the salt mines. I had so many questions about who she was and her people. How many of them were there? Where had they come from? Had they always lived in the Underland? But most of all, how had this world existed without anyone knowing about it? "Do you know other City people?"

Ama's frown deepened. "Krux."

I glanced at Ren. "We know Krux too," he said.

Her eyes grew wide with fear.

I tried to imagine how I would feel in Ama's shoes. Terrified, probably. I softened my face and smiled. "I'm Sari and this is Ren. We're not going to hurt you. We're just"—I searched for the right word—"exploring."

Ama frowned with confusion, like she was trying to decide if she should trust me or not. Like any child, her emotions showed clearly on her face.

"Me too."

"Did you find anything interesting?"

She stared at me and then shook her head. "I was looking for Jacob."

My heart beat faster. The pieces were starting to fit. Sy had said I had to go deeper to find the answers and he was right. This Underlander knew Kaia's birth elder. "Why are you looking for him?"

Ama pressed her lips together, refusing to talk. She pulled her knees tighter into her chest. "I'm not supposed to be out here. I need to get back to the pit," she whispered. "But I don't know where it is."

"I do," I said. "We can help you find it. But first, can you tell me about Jacob?"

"He's gone. Krux took him."

"Why did Krux take him?" Ren asked.

Ama shrugged. Everywhere else, she was skin and bones, but her shoulders were bulky, disproportionate from the rest of her. "We don't know. Old Father's angry. He's been rumbling since Jacob left."

"Who's Old Father? Is that an overseer?"

Ama frowned at Ren. "He's no person. He's ancient and everywhere. Right here in these rocks, even in the air we breathe. Big Mother can't protect us from him, not when he shakes the ground and splits the ceiling open. Rocks tumble down and there's no getting away."

"The tremors," Ren whispered to me.

"You think when the ground shakes, it's because Old Father's mad?" I asked.

Ama nodded.

"What if you stopped digging? Could you do that?" Ren asked.

Ama looked at him like he was an imbecile. "Then we don't eat. We only get food when the digging's done."

"Can you take us to the pit?" Ren asked.

I shook my head at Ren. "I don't think that's a good idea," I said quietly. "Imagine if some Prims showed up in the City unannounced?" He caught my meaning and nodded. "Ama, can you tell your people about us? Let them know we want to help? We're going to come back another time. Maybe we can figure out how to help Old Father not be so mad."

Ama kept staring at us, like she was memorizing every detail. "If you want to go back to the pit, take that tunnel. It'll lead you right to it." I pointed her in the right direction.

She stood up and slipped on her headlamp. Ren and I both watched as she scuttled away towards the pit. Part of me couldn't believe we'd found her. Underlanders existed! But another part, a bigger part, was sickened at the thought that a whole group of people were living in the dark and no one knew.

No, that wasn't true. At least one person in the City did know about them: Krux. And if he knew, others must too. They were digging for someone, after all. The question was: who?

Ama

I *met City people.* The words kept echoing in my head. Krux had lied when he told us Unders City people wanted to hurt us. They didn't, at least not Sari and Ren. They wanted to help us.

I raced back the way they'd told me to go. Soon as I got my first whiff of the pit, I wanted to cry with relief. The darkness yawned in front of me and I fell to my knees and thanked Big Mother for sending me the City people and Old Father for not rumbling while I was in the tunnels.

I turned off my headlamp. Everyone would be asleep, and I didn't want to wake them. I tiptoed past Noah's empty station. He'd be working on the escape tunnel, probably wondering where I was. I got a little twist of guilt in my gut. But after everything I'd seen, I needed to lie down and sort it out.

"Where were you?"

I nearly jumped out of my skin at the voice. Kibo! "You scared me," I said, swatting at him.

"You scared me!" he countered. "First Jacob, then Noah and now you! Why'd you leave the pit?" The whites of Kibo's eyes glistened in the dark. I was sorry to have scared him, and grateful that he hadn't woken Romi to ask where I was.

"Well?" he asked. "Where'd you go?"

"I went looking for Jacob."

His reaction was pretty much what I expected. "Are you crazy! Out *there*? What if Krux found you? Or—" The possibilities were too horrible. "Did Noah go with you?"

I stared at Kibo for a long time. Jacob had sworn me to secrecy, but I trusted Kibo almost as much as I trusted Romi. If we had his strong muscles helping us, we'd be able to finish the tunnel even faster. "He's not with me," I sighed. "But I know where he is."

Kibo shone the light in my face. "What's going on, Ama?"

The truth sat like a lump in my throat. "This way."

We tiptoed through the pit and to the opening to the pool. "Ama?" Kibo whispered. "Where are we going?"

"You have to trust me!"

We kept going. I ran my hand over Big Mother's rock, silently thanking her again for getting me back safely. The pool's turquoise water lit up with the headlamp's beam. "Over here," I said and pointed to the nearly hidden entrance to the cranny where the escape tunnel began. Dirt and rocks had trickled down the tunnel and lay in a pile. When he was done digging, Noah would push it into the pool. Kibo shone his headlamp first at the pile and then at me.

"We've been digging up," I told him.

He shook his head in disbelief. "How far does it go?"

"I don't know for sure. But you figure, we've been working on it instead of sleeping for so long…look at how far our tunnels go in the digging chambers."

"That's with all of us Unders digging. This tunnel got dug by just you."

"Not just me. Jacob too, and now Noah."

I could see Kibo doing the calculations and trying to figure it out. Was it long enough to get near to the surface? "Soon as we break though, all us Unders can leave."

Kibo blinked at me and I wondered if he hadn't heard me right. "Leave and go where?"

"To the Mountain. Where Jacob and Noah's people are."

I'd known Kibo since we were younguns in the nest. After Romi, he was the closest person to me, but the look on his face made me want to punch him. "Why would we go there?"

I didn't understand his question. "Why would we stay?"

"What about Old Father? He won't like that. Big Mother protects us *here*. This is our home. Out there we have no one looking out for us."

"Big Mother's going to protect us wherever we are." I truly believed that. There was no way she'd abandon us. But Old Father? I was never sure about him. Big Mother gave to us Unders, but all Old Father did was take. I needed a way to make Kibo see things my way. "Old Father's been letting Jacob and me dig this tunnel. You think he'd let us keep working on it if he didn't want us to leave?"

"But Jacob's gone, Ama! What if he got taken because Old Father didn't like what he was doing? Maybe he's with the other fathers right now."

What the mothers had told me about there being no fathers sat in the back of my mind. Was that true? If it was, what happened to all the boys who'd left the pit? What would happen to Kibo? "He's not with the fathers. There was no celebration. We didn't clap him out. Krux took him. You saw it the same as me." Kibo didn't have anything to say about that. "We don't know what happens to the fathers. They just leave. At least with the mothers, we know they're still around because we see the younguns."

Kibo put his hands on his hips and stared me down. "What are you saying, Ama?"

I took a breath. The only way he was gonna believe me was if I told him everything. "I found the mothers," I blurted.

Kibo's eyes widened and he gaped at me. "You did?"

"Yeah, but they're not what we think." Their skin didn't shimmer with light the way I'd thought it would. My heart didn't feel full being around them. "They live in a little room. Five of them together, crowded worse than we are. There's nothing special about them, Kibo, except some of them had round bellies. Otherwise, they're just like us."

Kibo shook his head. "No, they're not. They're the mothers."

"Kibo—" I started, but he was adamant.

"You left the pit. You broke one of the rules, so maybe what you saw is wrong. Maybe those weren't the mothers."

"Sela was there. And Valla." Hearing those words shut him up because he'd seen Krux take both of them away, same as me. I kept talking to get all my words out before he started arguing again. "The mothers told me about the fathers. Why would they lie?"

Kibo didn't have an answer. He pulled his eyebrows together. The headlamp on his forehead wobbled. Its light started to dim because we were standing still. "Old Father has his ways," was all Kibo said.

I was afraid to say out loud what I was thinking, not just because it was going to make Kibo mad. If I was wrong, Old Father wouldn't forgive me. I screwed up my courage though because I had to. I didn't want to carry this doubt around with me. "What if Old Father doesn't exist? Remember the stories about what happened when the first diggers got mad? It wasn't Old Father who took them. The City people killed them."

That started my head spinning in a different direction because I'd met City people. I thought of Sari's kind face. She wanted to help, not hurt.

Kibo didn't want to believe it. His face crunched up hard and he shook his head. "I think you're lying to make me leave with you."

"I wouldn't do that."

"You've been digging this tunnel with Jacob because *you* wanted to escape. You never said anything to anyone else. Never asked us what we wanted. You're always thinking about yourself."

"That's not true, Kibo!" His words were a blow. All this time, I'd been planning and hoping for the day we'd be free of the Underland, and here was Kibo telling me he didn't even want to go.

"I don't want to see your tunnel. If you want to leave the Underland, then leave, but don't drag the rest of us away."

"I'm not dragging—" I started, but Kibo didn't stick around to listen. He marched off, dodging the sleeping bodies, and lay down on his mat.

I slid down to the ground with my back against the wall. Tears leaked out of the corners of my eyes. What if it was all for nothing? What if Kibo was right and Jacob had been taken?

Or worse, what if everything I hoped for was just a lie?

—

I found my way back to my sleeping mat and nestled in close to Romi. Her breathing was so deep and peaceful. I tried to match it, but everything about me was too jumpy. I kept spinning backwards from my talk with Kibo, to meeting the City people, to the Mothers.

"Ama?" Romi asked, rolling over. "You okay?"

There was no point lying, Romi knew me too well. It'd be like lying to myself. I wiggled even closer so my breath was her breath and told her everything, from the moment I stepped out of the pit, to the second I lay down beside her.

Her breathing wasn't deep and peaceful when I was done. "If we leave, everything's gonna change," she said.

"It's changing no matter what. Stay or go, it's not safe here. For lots of reasons," I added. She knew what I meant. Her bleeds were gonna take her away from me.

"At least here, we know who we are. The pit is our home. Leaving to be a mother isn't as scary as leaving the Underland."

"You don't know what you're saying, Romi."

"Neither do you!" She lowered her voice when Luken mumbled in his sleep. "I'm not saying I won't go with you, but what if where we go is worse?"

"Jacob wouldn't lead us somewhere worse." But even as I said it, doubts squeezed into my head like beetles under a rock. *First Kibo, and now Romi*, I grumbled to myself. I shifted away from Romi. I didn't want to be wrong, but more than that, I didn't want them to be right.

Romi grabbed my hand. Deep in the tunnels, a shake started. The rumble and crash of rock echoed in the pit. "You see," Romi said, "he's warning you. Old Father knows."

Sari

I took a deep gulp of air when I got to the surface. Ren's shift started right away, so he went one way and I went directly to the changeroom in the gymnasium. A few females milled around, chatting on the benches or heading to the shower area. Their conversation stopped, as it always did, when an overseer was present.

I found a quiet spot, took off the overseer uniform and hung it on a hook. Underneath, my tunic was damp with sweat. That came off too and I went to the showers. I wanted to sink to the floor when the warm mist hit my skin. The fog of water vapor made a cloud and I couldn't see who stepped to the nozzle beside me until she spoke. "Sari?" It was Mika. "I was watching for you. You were gone a long time," she said.

I went through the motions of washing myself, but all I could think about was what I'd seen and who was beneath my feet.

"We met someone," I said. Through the steam I mouthed the word *"Underlander"* to Mika. Her eyes widened for a moment, then she concealed her surprise as two females took stations near us. The mist quietly died as my time ran out and I was left shivering in the humid air. "We talked to her," I said quietly. I thought Mika was going to fall over.

We got changed quickly. Mika tucked the overseer uniform I'd worn into the bottom of her shopping basket. "Let's go. We need to find a place to talk."

"I have to get to the clinic. Walk with me?"

We stuck close to the stream and kept our voices low. Mika demanded I tell her everything. "Your theories are right. The MAP is accurate—or almost accurate. There's a pit, and digging tunnels."

"I knew it," Mika muttered. "And the Underlander?"

"Her name's Ama. She looked young, small too, but strong. We met her in a tunnel. She was lost. She knew about the City. She said they dig for us and that's how they get food." I broke off, shaking my head. "It's like from Before when people were forced to work and treated terribly."

How could the Council allow this to go on? "She's going to tell the others about us. Ren and I are going back."

"Why? We have the information we need."

I shook my head. I didn't think that was true. "She talked about a Prim named Jacob."

"A Prim? How would an Underlander know a Prim?"

I explained what I'd learned from Sy and Mae about Kaia, and how Sy had told me to 'go deeper' to find the answers about why Kaia had left. "I need to figure out how it's all connected. Maybe it'll explain why Kaia left."

Mika walked beside me quietly. Probably digesting everything I'd told her. "And the tremors? Did you ask her about those?"

"They think the tremors happen because the rocks are mad at them. It didn't make sense to me. She panicked when Ren told her to stop digging."

"You and Ren have to tell everything to Avi and Dex. And then, we'll decide what to do next."

We parted ways, me to start my shift at the clinic and Mika to go back into the Underland for her work. As I watched her leave, I got a twinge in my chest. She of all people knew how dangerous it was underground. She didn't just have herself to worry about anymore.

⌒

"I think we should go to the Council. Tell them what you saw."

I looked at Avi. Something about him still bothered me. Was it his shifty eyes? Or the way he stared at me for a beat too long, as if he were trying to decide if *I* could be trusted. "Telling the Council could get us balanced." I shot a look at Mika, who nodded in agreement. The five of us were eating dinner together again, our heads bent over plates of salad. The lettuce was bitter, but no one complained. I barely tasted it anyway. "The Council are the ones who have kept the Underland a secret. Who knows what they're willing to do to keep it that way?"

"There might be a reason—" Avi started, but I cut him off.

"There's no reason to let someone be treated like that. You didn't see her. She was half-starved. Barely clothed." I looked around the communal kitchen area. Everyone was wearing clean tunics, their plates full. They got to sleep in a warm, comfortable bed. What did Ama eat? Where did she sleep? What kind of a life was it for her in the Underland?

"It's not just about the Underlanders," I said. All eyes turned to me. "The tremors are getting stronger. Ama was scared. She knows they're in danger."

"If there's a major cave-in, they'll be trapped down there. They could all die." Mika spoke with authority. "If other Citizens knew the truth—"

"They'd do nothing," Ren interrupted.

"That's not true," I argued, shocked at his harsh words. "If people knew about the Underlanders they'd demand better treatment for them."

"Better, but not equal. Think about it, Sari. Would you go into the pit to dig brine? Because you'd have to if you want our way of life to stay the same." Ren dropped his voice, but the crease between his eyebrows remained. "I've thought about it all day. Even if the whole City knew about the Underlanders, they wouldn't care."

"I don't think that's true. We care." I looked at the four other faces staring back at me. Mika nodded in agreement, so did Dex. I turned to Avi. "Don't we?"

"Ren is right. I wouldn't go down there. I worked hard to get where I am. Why should I give it up? The Underlanders are down there for a reason. Maybe they're not fit for anything other than digging. I mean, we're here because of our genetics. Just like the Prims are on the Mountain because of theirs."

As Avi spoke, I realized what it was about him that set me on edge. He thought he was better than the rest of us. Sure, his job required more schooling than mine. He'd probably scored higher on his intellectual aptitude tests, but that didn't make him an expert on the Underland, or its people. He wasn't the one who'd gone down there, I was. That had to count for something.

"Let's just say the Underlanders stopped digging. Where would they live? In the dwelling next to you? Or would we make them go outside? It's a lose-lose situation for everyone. It's better if they stay down there. They've never known a different life anyway. They won't know what they're missing. After so long, genetically, they're more efficient at digging than you or I would be." Avi spoke as if his word was the final say on the subject.

"What about their safety? You heard what Mika said," I whispered urgently. "If there's a cave-in, they'll be trapped."

"Which means we lose our energy source anyway," Dex finished. He gave Avi a pointed look.

Avi surveyed us coolly and motioned with his chin to the figures behind me. "Keep your voice down," he said. Two overseers had stationed themselves at the entrance to the kitchen.

"Are they here for us?" I asked.

Dex shook his head. "No. Your pulse points were scrambled. There's no way they know where you were."

I glanced at Ren. He looked as worried as I was. But there was no denying the more than occasional glances they threw our way. Or was it my imagination? Were they scrutinizing every table?

Avi stood up abruptly. "You're on your own."

"Avi," Ren said warningly. "You know the deal. We're in this together."

Dex put a hand on Avi's arm and squeezed until Avi winced and sat down. "Ren's right. You can't back out now."

Avi shot a look at the overseers. "You can't tell me what I can do. This started with questions, that's it. I just wanted to know where the extra energy came from. Now I know. I never wanted to change the way the City runs. You think the four of you are strong enough to go against the Council?" he shook his head. "You're fighting a losing battle."

This time, when he stood up, no one stopped him. "This isn't a game anymore."

"It never was," Ren hissed.

"Don't contact me again."

"What if he goes to an overseer?" I asked as he left the kitchen. He walked past the overseers at the entrance and I held my breath.

"If he tells them what we did…" I let my voice trail off. We'd all be implicated. Ren and I for going into the Underland, Dex for scrambling the pulse points, and Mika for knowing all of it and doing nothing.

Dex shook his head. "I've known Avi since we were in school. He wouldn't do that to us. He's scared, that's all."

"So am I," Mika said. "We all are. Knowing the truth is a burden," she said ruefully. She looked at the Citizens still in the kitchen. At the table next to us two birth elders were eating dinner with their toddler. They grinned at the child who was happily chomping on a carrot. Mika sighed and glanced at Dex. "Now that we do, we have to take action." Ren met my eyes. "We need a plan."

I tapped my fingers on the table, thinking.

"I think Avi's right, people won't care unless they know how it affects them," I said.

"The dome caving in will affect everyone," Mika said.

"But no one on the surface can feel the tremors yet," Ren said. "I've only felt small vibrations in the Underland. Nothing that's made me think the dome could come down."

"Just wait," Mika said, ominously. "A big one's coming."

It was hard to believe the people who were supposed to lead us would risk the City to protect a secret. Did they have a plan? Or were they turning a blind eye to the truth because they didn't like it. Maybe they didn't understand just how much danger we were in. Or maybe the change to our way of life wasn't worth it. I hated to think that our leaders would be so foolish, but I knew it had happened Before. That was why we were living in a dome now—no one had taken the warnings about the environment and disease seriously back then either.

"What if we could show Citizens what the tremors are like in the Underland?" I asked. "Ama was definitely scared of them.

We could go to the pit, wait until one hit and store the footage in our memory." I looked at Dex. "Could you upload it onto the newsfeed?"

Dex frowned. "That's not my department. I'd have to figure out a way into the system."

"But you could do it?"

"I could try."

I looked around the table, the plan solidifying in my mind. "The Council won't be able to lie if we have proof. Even if Citizens don't care about the way the Underlanders are being treated, they can't ignore the tremors."

It was strange to look at Mika, Dex and Ren and know they were listening to me, willing to take direction from me. How had I ended up in this position? Kaia would never have believed it. "We'll go tomorrow. Right after my shift at the clinic."

"And if there aren't any tremors?" Mika asked.

"Then we keep going, night after night until we're there for one. What choice do we have?" Until that moment, I hadn't understood why Kaia had willingly risked her safety to find her birth elder. It was clear to me now. The truth had changed her. She couldn't go on living a lie in the City. And neither could I.

The two overseers wandered closer to our table. "Meet me in the square at six o'clock tomorrow," I said to Ren and stood to go.

"Where are you going?" he asked. "You didn't touch your dinner."

"I'm not hungry. You can have it." He opened his mouth to say something more, but I turned away. The overseers were watching me. The faster I could get away from the table, the better.

I walked aimlessly along the stream, following the meandering path until I ended up in the orchard. The smell of citrus and freshly turned soil greeted me. Brightly coloured fruit dotted the foliage. The trees stood in even rows, their branches carefully pruned so they made a canopy. It was strange to be here by myself. The orchard was the unofficial place for young couples, both matched and unmatched, to meet.

The last time I'd been here had been with Lev. I flushed with embarrassment at the memory of it. Kaia had been reeling from Mae's balancing and I'd been thinking about myself. I couldn't fix what I'd done. I found an empty bench and sat down. I needed space to think.

Now that I knew the truth about Kaia, I didn't want her to come back. I knew why Tar wanted her and it turned my stomach. Tar's moral ambiguity might have allowed her to trade the life of one person to save many, but mine didn't.

I loved Kaia. If it came down to saving her, or all the Citizens, I'd choose her. I'd been selfish when Mae had been taken. When she'd needed me most, I'd failed her. More than anything, I wished I could go back and prove to Kaia I could be a good friend. If I'd been the person she needed, she wouldn't have left, Lev wouldn't have been sent after her and Mae wouldn't still be trapped in a cell.

My eyes flew open. I knew what Kaia would want me to do. She couldn't help Mae, but I could.

"Great minds think alike." I jumped at the voice and looked up to see Ren smiling down at me. "Mind if I join you?" he asked.

As distracted as I was by thoughts of Mae and Kaia, I didn't say no. Ren settled in beside me, close enough that I could sense his warmth, but far enough away to be appropriate. I still had a mate, after all. A few couples strolled along the path between the trees. We were tucked far enough away not to draw attention. "I was worried about you. You seemed upset when you left. I wanted to make sure it wasn't with me."

"No," I said, shaking my head. "Of course not."

He sighed with relief. "Good. Are you nervous about going back?"

"That's part of it," I admitted. "I was wishing I could go back in time and do things differently."

"You mean your match with Lev?" he asked.

I nodded. "Other things too. Things I should have said or done. Maybe Kaia would have stayed."

"I know you regret that she left, but that was Kaia's choice, not yours. If she hadn't gone, you wouldn't be part of the CORE. We wouldn't be talking about saving the City, or the Underlanders. There's some good that's come of it."

We sat in comfortable silence for a few moments. But thoughts of the Underland and what would happen tomorrow were never far from my mind. "We should have a plan in case we get separated in the Underland. Or if one of us gets hurt." I'd seen the fear on Ama's face when we'd mentioned the tremors. I wondered what they felt like so deep underground. "Nothing should compromise our goal. We need that footage otherwise things won't change. All our work will be for nothing."

"Okay," he agreed. "We keep going. No matter what."

We sat together for a while longer, then I stood to go. "You're leaving?" he asked.

I was feeling the effects of missing dinner. My stomach grumbled for food. If I left now, I'd make it to the market before it closed. "See you tomorrow," I said wiping the dirt off my tunic.

"I should go too," he said and stretched. He looked at his pulse point and rolled his eyes. "There's a running mat with my name on it."

I glanced back at Ren as he went towards the gymnasium. If Kaia hadn't left, I wouldn't have found Ren. Could we have a future together? Lev had to be declared dead for that to happen. I wasn't ready to give up yet. There was still a chance, a small sliver of hope, that he and Kaia were out there.

Ama

For many years, the Unders lived and worked in the Underland. But something was changing in the Underland. Old Father was getting angrier. His grumbles shook the ground. He roared too, so the ceiling cracked open. The Underland was getting more dangerous, but where could the Unders go? This was their home.

The Unders knew about the City people. But it turned out, the City people had forgotten about the Unders. They'd been in the Underland for so long that they'd disappeared from the City people's memory. Until a City person and an Under met.

The City person was clean and shimmery like Big Mother, only without the belly. The dirt of the Underland didn't stick to her. She told the Underlander she wanted to help. She was worried about the tremors. She knew something had to be done. She promised the Underlander she'd be back.

And the Underlander believed her because even in the darkest dark of the Underland, there can be a glimmer of hope. Maybe this City person had been sent by Big Mother. Maybe this City person could protect them from Old Father's anger and undo all the wrongs.

Maybe this City person could save them.

When I was done telling my story, Lila spoke first. "Is it true, Ama?" Her old eyes were tired. "The City people want to help?"

"It's what she said. There were two of them, but it was the girl who promised. She said she was coming back to help us."

"Krux says City people only want to hurt us," Kibo spoke up. "How can we trust her?"

I didn't know how to answer Kibo.

"We can't." Noah's gruff voice echoed off the pit. "You can't trust any City person."

"What's the harm in meeting with her?" Lila said. "They

need us to dig for them. Maybe she will help." I gave Lila a grateful smile. Romi stayed quiet, like usual.

But then, she reached over to squeeze my hand and it felt like a shout.

"She's coming back either way," I said, making my voice big. "She isn't the first stranger to be sent to us." I looked right at Noah. "And that worked out alright."

Lila snorted with laughter. "She's got you there, Noah."

He grumbled but didn't argue. "Get to your *mah*," he said. "And then into the tunnels. City person or not, we still gotta eat."

We all did as he said, but this *mah* felt different. I opened my mouth wide and let the sound pour out of me. The light inside of me glowed in a different way. It wasn't calm and peaceful; it was full of excitement and promise.

Sari

"Sari?" An overseer stood outside my dwelling. I looked up and down the walkway. Citizens strolled past, on their way home from work, or off to the kitchen for their evening meal.

"Yes," I nodded and tried to keep my breathing even. The overseer's uniform, evidence of my guilt, was tucked into my satchel. I pressed the bag closer to me. He didn't look like the enforcer type of overseer, the ones who would have questioned Sy and left him bruised and bloodied. This one looked too mild-mannered to do any damage.

"You're being reassigned," he said. "To the Singles Complex."

"Oh." My voice trembled with relief. I covered it by clearing my throat.

"In light of you being Lev's mate, we thought it best to deliver the news in person in case you had any questions. If he should come back, you would move back into a couple's unit, of course."

"When do I need to be out?" I sighed.

"In five days. It's usually three, but Councillor Tar arranged for an extension."

Councillor Tar? "How considerate of her." The overseer nodded and walked away. He was an average Citizen. Probably had an average mate and one child. He went about his day, working, going to the gymnasium, and taking his meals at the communal kitchen. He had no idea what was going on below his feet, or the corrupt system that allowed it to happen.

I couldn't figure out if I was jealous of him, or if I pitied him.

I walked to our meeting spot and right on time, Ren arrived. "Ready?" he asked as we walked towards the stairs that led into the Underland. I nodded. My mouth was too dry to speak.

I'd thought ahead this time and had filled my satchel with a gourd of water and some food. We could be down there all night waiting for a tremor. The satchel was slung across one shoulder and sat on the opposite hip. Its weight was comforting. Ren noticed the bag, and I held up the gourd by way of explanation. He nodded. "Good thinking." Besides the food and water, there was something else in my satchel. A knife. It lay in the bottom of the bag wrapped in a cloth. I'd taken it from the kitchen on my way to meet Ren. I didn't tell him about the knife because it wasn't for me, it was for Mae and Sy.

"Evening, Ren," an overseer at the bottom of the stairs said. She looked at me and tilted her head. "Are you new?"

My breath caught in my throat. "Storage room," I blurted and held up my satchel. "We need to return some supplies." She gave us the once over, so I leaned towards her and dropped my voice, "I'm already on my supervisor's bad side. If he realizes I forgot to do it..."

She gave me a knowing look and nodded for me to go ahead. We moved through the corridor. Late at night, the Councillor's chambers were all empty. Another overseer walked towards us. I kept my eyes forward and picked up my pace, as if we were in a rush to get somewhere.

The fabric under my arms was damp with sweat as I passed Mae's cell and then Sy's. "Ren," I whispered and tilted my head toward the cell's open door. I asked the question with my eyes. *Was he balanced?*

Ren nodded. "This afternoon," he said. "I'm sorry."

"And Mae?"

He shook his head. "Not yet."

My chest tightened. How much longer would she be alive? Hours? Days? I said a silent goodbye to Sy as we continued down the corridor.

The ceiling cut-outs disappeared and the tunnels narrowed. Ren had a lightstick at the ready, but I had to dig into the satchel to find mine. My fingers brushed against the handle of the knife at the bottom of the bag. The corridor turned, sloping downhill. Even with the lightstick, I had to put one hand along the wall to make sure I didn't lose my footing.

Ren held up a hand for me to stop and made a slicing motion across his neck. I let my lightstick die and pressed myself against the wall. He crept forward. I saw what he'd seen. A light shone from an intersecting corridor. It bounced up and down with someone's footsteps.

If the person kept walking straight, we wouldn't be noticed, but if the person turned, they'd find us. There was nowhere to hide; no nearby tunnels to tuck ourselves into. We were too far into the Underland for any excuses.

I watched the beam of light fill up the tunnel as it grew closer. We had the element of surprise on our side. Ren shuffled forward, pressing his back against the wall. The person was almost at the intersection when Ren slipped around the corner and disappeared from view. There was a scuffle and a gasp, then a sizzling sound, which I knew was a taser. One of them had gotten a jolt. *Please don't let it be Ren.* As much as I wanted to check, I couldn't risk exposing myself. I stayed huddled against the wall. My heart hammered in my chest, but it wasn't loud enough to block out the sound of a body being dragged away.

Further in the Underland, a door shut and I was left in complete darkness, and alone.

I waited for Ren to return. To hear his familiar footsteps, or some signal that let me know he was okay. There was nothing.

Timidly, I squeezed the handle of my lightstick and watched as the glow lit up my feet and the walls around me. Staying where I was wasn't an option. We'd agreed on a plan if something happened to one of us. It had made sense on the surface, but now that it had happened, I was paralyzed with indecision. I didn't want to abandon Ren. I wanted to race back towards the surface and alert the other CORE members. I took a deep, steadying breath. Ren knew the risk, I reasoned. If I left, our plan would fail.

Blood pounded in my ears.

I pushed myself away from the dirt wall and darted past the intersection. It was pitched in darkness. There was no evidence that Ren had ever been there.

I'll come back, I promised. But first, I needed to complete what we started. I needed to find the Underlanders.

Being alone in the Underland was far scarier than when I'd been with Ren. I jumped at every stone that skittered under my feet. I kept second-guessing myself. Had I gone too far? Taken a wrong turn? I pulled up the MAP repeatedly to check it.

But then the odour of human stench hit me and I knew I was getting closer. I paused and lowered the lightstick so its beam fell on the floor. I crept forward. Ahead of me the tunnel veered right. A few more steps and I'd be in the pit.

One step.

Two steps.

Three steps.

I turned the corner and held up my lightstick. Its beam dissolved into the darkness of an open space. There was a fearful murmur and a sea of faces turned towards me.

I'd found them.

There was a shuffling noise as they hid in the shadows and tucked themselves against the cave walls. None of them wanted to be seen. I remembered what Ama had said, how she worried I'd hurt her. I raised my hands to show I carried no weapon.

"Who are you?" I jumped at the voice. It was deep and raspy. I turned the lightstick toward the sound. A male with white hair and beard moved towards me. "Who are you?" he asked again. I squinted into the lightstick's glare.

I guess I'd thought the Underlanders would react more like Ama had, worried and fearful. Shocked at my appearance. This male was hostile. Could he be a Prim? He was gruff and unkempt, but considering the living conditions, that wasn't surprising. A wild, scraggly beard hung down his chest.

It took all my resolve not to step back and shrink into the tunnel. "Sari," I said. "My name is Sari."

"Ama!" his voice boomed. From out of the darkness, a tiny figure appeared. "This her?"

Ama threw him a triumphant smile. "Yes! See, Noah! I told you she'd come."

Noah let out a long exhalation. "Why are you here? Who sent you?"

"No one sent me. I came to help."

"No City person ever wanted to help Unders before. Why now?"

I looked at the sea of faces. They'd inched away from the cave walls waiting for me to speak. Their lives were confined to the pit and the tunnels. The Underlanders had never seen trees or felt sunlight. All they knew was darkness and rock. What would happen to them when they got to the surface? My eyes had been opened to life in the Underland. What would it be like for them to see the City for the first time? "It's too dangerous for you to stay in the Underland. You have to stop digging."

There was a flurry of activity as the Unders turned to each other, whispering. Ama looked at Noah and then at me. She crossed her arms over her chest. "I tried telling some of them, but they didn't want to listen."

"If we stop digging, we won't get food," someone shouted. He moved his way to the front and stood beside Ama. He was young too, but taller and more sinewy than Ama, who was just skin and bones except for her bulky shoulders. "As long as the brine gets to you, what goes on here doesn't matter."

"If you don't stop, the tunnels will cave in. The dome that protects the City will crumble," I said.

Noah let out a raucous laugh. "Oh no! What will you City people do then?" His sarcasm set me on edge. "You might have to live outside!"

I glared at him. "I'm risking my life being here. I came with someone else, but he got taken." My voice shook as I remembered the sound of the taser's sizzle. "In the tunnels, someone grabbed him."

"Probably Krux," Noah said. "He's the only other person who comes down here." He surveyed me with narrowed eyes. "I don't trust City people. *Any City people.* We don't need your help." He walked away, leaving me standing in the entrance to the pit. Others hesitated, staring at me, but a few followed him.

I had to do something. "No one knows you even exist!" I

shouted. "You're a secret!" That made him stop, but he didn't turn around. I stared at his back.

"Where do they think the brine comes from?" Ama asked, curious.

"Citizens think we produce enough energy to power our City. They don't know about the brine. The Council lies to keep you a secret." I had their attention now. I kept talking, my words spilling out of my mouth. "People need to know the truth."

The Underlanders lived in the dark, but so did the Citizens. Noah turned around. "You're one person. No one's going listen to you. As long as the brine gets to the City, no one cares what goes on down here." He fixed Ama with a meaningful look. "We don't need her help."

Ama looked at me expectantly. I couldn't just leave. "Yes, you do! It's not safe down here. The tremors that shake your tunnels are getting worse, aren't they?"

There was a long silence. "What if they are?" Noah growled.

"The tunnels aren't stable. They could collapse. The pit too," I looked up at the ceiling of the room we were in.

"And how are you going to help us?" Noah understood how much danger they were in. I could see it on his face; he was scared.

"First, I need proof. That you exist and that the tremors start here. Once I have that, no one will be able to deny the truth." I pulled up the hologram from my pulse point. A shimmery square filled the air in front of me. I ignored the gasps and muffled screams and swiped to open the images I'd saved of them as we'd been talking. Ama gaped. "That's us!"

"I'll send images of you back to the City. Citizens will see how you live. They'll understand the danger we're in and that something has to be done. They won't stand for it once they know the truth."

Ama

I stared at the girl called Sari. In the dim light, her skin glowed. She was cleaner that I'd ever be. She looked so special that I knew Big Mother had sent her. She didn't even look like the same kind of creature as us Unders.

I raised my nose to get a sniff. She didn't smell like anything I knew. The damp of the cave hadn't sunk into her. She was crisp smelling; that was the best way to describe how her scent sat sharp in my nose. I moved closer without even knowing I was doing it. Romi tugged at my tunic, trying to hold me back.

When the wavy reflection shot out of her finger, we all gasped. She called it an image. She was capturing us even as we stood in front of her. I touched my arms and my face to make sure it wasn't a trick; that I hadn't been sucked into that picture. "It saves what we see," Sari said. "And I can share it with the other City people."

"Bring her into the pit, Ama," Lila said, stepping up. "We can show her how it is down here."

Noah didn't move or speak. He stood still as a rock, but I saw the grumbling on his face. He didn't like having this City person here. She came offering help, we couldn't say we didn't need it. Just look at us! 'Course we did!

Lila brought Sari further into the pit and lifted her arms like it was something to see. "This here is where we all live."

"All together?" Sari asked.

"'Cept for the younguns who stay in the nest."

"And the Mothers," I said. "They got their own place, a room to themselves."

"*Mothers*," Sari murmured to herself. "And the males?"

"They go to Old Father," Kibo said, his voice big and proud. I gritted my teeth and gave him a sharp look.

"But we don't know where that is," I fired back. "Krux takes them and we never see them again."

"Because they're with Old Father," Kibo insisted. Now wasn't the time to be arguing, so I let it go. I'd told Kibo what I'd learned from the mothers. If he'd been there with me, maybe he'd think differently. Sari's face changed when she looked around, like she had a question she wasn't sure she should ask. "Where do you cook? And eat?"

"All right here," Lila said. Seemed kind of obvious to me.

"And sleep too," Sari guessed looking at the sleeping mats. That's when she turned around and really looked at all of us. I wished I knew what was going on in her head.

"What's it like up where you live?" I asked. I was the only one brave enough to ask about the City. The rest of them just looked like their mouths were filled with rock dust.

Sari didn't get a chance to answer because the sudden rumble under our feet made everyone hush. It wasn't like we weren't used to it, but every time the quaking started, we didn't know how long it was gonna last. The younguns held onto each other or rushed to Lila. Deep down in the tunnels, there was a crack. It was just instinct that made me turn and look for Romi. There she was with a crowd of younguns, Luken included, clinging to her.

When the shaking stopped, all us Unders looked around relieved. It wasn't much of anything to us, but Sari stood trembling. "Is that what they're all like?" she asked.

"Worse if you're in a tunnel," Kibo said. "Old Father likes reminding us he's in charge."

She looked up at the ceiling like it might come crashing down on her. "You can't stay here," she said.

I glanced at Sari. She wasn't here to hurt us; I was sure of it. What would she say when she found out we'd been working on a plan to leave the Underland all this time?

I caught Noah's eye. A secret question passed from me to him. *Should we tell her about the escape tunnel?* He shook his head with a fierce look warning me to keep my mouth shut. He was never going to trust a City person.

Sari

The vibration I'd felt that day in the corridor was nothing like the shaking in the Underland. The crack of rocks sounded like thunder. I needed to get back to the surface to share the images. Mika had made it clear we were in danger, and she was right. Once Dex had the images, we'd make a plan to get Ren.

I bent down so I could look Ama in the eye. "I have to go," I told her. "I need to show my friends what it's like down here." I adjusted the satchel on my shoulder. Its weight reminded me of the things I'd brought for her. I dug the tomatoes out of my satchel. "Here, these are from the City."

"What are they?" Ama asked.

"Tomatoes," Noah said, gruffly. But I was sure his voice cracked just a bit.

I gave her a handful of shiny green things. "And these?"

"Peapods," he said wistfully. I glanced at Noah from the corner of my eye. He wasn't here by choice. He was a captive. No wonder he hated City people.

"I'll be back," I promised Ama.

Before I left, I glanced once more at the faces of the Underlanders behind her; the rags they wore and their tattered sleeping mats. They lived in squalor that was unimaginable in the City and it was the Council's doing.

I kept my lightstick on its dimmest setting as I moved through the tunnels. My ears were pricked for any noise. Whoever had taken Ren might still be down here. Pausing before I got to the spot where he'd been taken, I pulled the knife out of my satchel. Better to be safe than sorry.

The corridor was clear. There was no sign of Krux, or Ren. I kept walking. Further along, I came to Mae's cell. It was still locked by the bar which meant she was alive, at least for now. Would she go along with my plan? Did I have time to put it into action? Ren had been taken and I had images to share with Dex. Sneaking into Mae's cell would delay things. I hesitated, torn by my loyalties.

Two overseers turned into the corridor. I hid in a corridor adjacent to it, my heart pounding, and waited until they moved past.

I'd agreed to be part of the CORE because I wanted things in the City to be different, the truth about what really went on down here needed to be revealed, and that included the mistreatment of an original inhabitant. I couldn't leave the Underland without helping Mae.

I waited until the corridor was empty and went to the door and slid the bar back. "Mae?" I called out. I kept my voice low and shone my lightstick inside the cell.

"Sari?" Mae was sitting against the wall. She shielded her face from the light. I took a few more steps inside and shut the door. The cell seemed smaller than I remembered it.

"How are you?"

She looked more defeated than she had the last time. She was losing hope.

"Sy's gone," I said.

She gave a miserable nod. "I figured. I wonder if he understood what was happening. His mind..." Mae's voice drifted off. Then, she sighed. "This isn't how I imagined my last days."

"That's why I'm here." I moved closer to her. "I want to help." I pulled the knife out of my satchel. Mae brought her hands away from her face and stared at the blade. Her breath caught in her throat. "You don't have do things their way."

"I can't fight back," she said. "Look at me."

"That's not why I brought this."

Her eyes widened in understanding. "I can't do that either," she said.

"So you'd rather wait for Krux to come back and drag you away?" I didn't understand. Wouldn't it be better to end things on her own terms?

"No," Mae looked at me and shook her head. "I want to go back to the City and show the Citizens how the Council treats its oldest members. The death they promise isn't honorable. How many others have been held like this? As if we don't matter. As if we're nothing."

If I led Mae back into the City, I'd be caught and then it would be me sitting in one of these cells. I gulped, weighing my options. I was here for Kaia as much as for Mae. But was what she was asking too much? It put the CORE at risk too.

But with Ren taken, maybe the CORE was already compromised. If he talked, all our names would be known. This might be my only chance to do something.

Bits of dried mud sprinkled down from the ceiling. A larger chunk came loose and fell to the floor at my feet. It took me a moment to realize what was happening. "Mae!" She stood up and moved towards me as another tremor ripped through the Underland. This one was much stronger. I had to hold on to the wall to keep balanced. Mae covered her head with her hands. There were shouts from closer to the entrance.

If I'd been doubting taking her to the City with me before, the force of the tremor changed all that.

There was a burst of static on my newsfeed and a message came through. I was back online, which meant Dex had unscrambled my locator. "Prim Threat Level is Extreme. Find safety. We are under attack," the newsfeed voice said in my ear.

The messages I'd missed while I was in the Underland came through. They were all from Mika. *Where are you? Get back. NOW!* And the final one: *The baby.*

I opened the door a crack and scanned the corridor. Two overseers rushed past, headed for the City. I had to act quickly. At least if the City was in panic, Mae might go unnoticed. For a while anyway. "Come on, Mae," I held the knife in my hand. It was the only weapon I had. Would I be able to use it if someone came at us? There was another rumble. More dirt and dust shook loose from the ceiling. I waved my hand in front of me to clear the air. When I did, we weren't alone. Another figure stood in the corridor, blocking our way.

Ama

After Sari left, Noah called me to his station. "You're not digging today," he said to me. "Not for brine anyway." His face was stony. He turned to the entrance to the pool, where the escape tunnel was hidden. "We're close, Ama."

"But Sari," I said. "She'll be back—"

Noah cut me off. "We don't need her."

I frowned at him. "How can you be sure? We don't know what's out there. Or where Jacob is. What if Sari can help us?"

"Listen to me, Ama. There is nothing we want from a City person. Understand? You and Jacob dug this tunnel and it's you who's gonna lead us out of here." Hearing Noah sound so sure made my stomach flip. "Go tell your team you're not digging with them this shift."

I did as Noah said, but I didn't like seeing my team move into the tunnels without me. *Keep them safe, Big Mother,* I thought.

Kibo looked back at me like he was giving me one more chance to change my mind. I shook my head. It was too late for that.

Once all the teams were gone, I went to meet Noah at the cranny. He had all our supplies. "You go first," Noah said. I put on my headlamp, grabbed a digging hammer, and hauled myself into the tunnel. I shimmied my way up into that rock and felt Old Father all around me, holding me tight.

But it was Big Mother I thought about. How she was looking out for me, filling me up with being brave so I could help all her children; the younguns and the mothers. I listened hard to the rocks, waiting for them to whisper her stories. I thought about how us Unders were trapped. Down here, there was no room to stretch out. The boys got taken before they could be fully grown and the girls who became mothers were trapped in a tiny cell. We were like the trees Jacob told me about. They had roots, but it was what happened when they broke through the earth that made them special. They drank up the water that fell from the sky and the light from the sun. We were like those trees. Our roots were in the rock, but we'd grow tall once we broke through.

That was what I was thinking about when the dust crumbled down on me. It wasn't rock; it was light and flaky. The next whack of my hammer loosened big chunks that skittered over my face. I leaned back and took another swing. This time, my axe didn't bounce back, it stuck. I gave it a yank and when I looked up, it wasn't more rock that I saw.

It was light.

"Noah!" I looked beneath me where he was chipping away the rock to make the tunnel wider. "Noah!"

"What?"

I squished myself up against the side so he could see. "We did it. We made it to the surface."

Noah whispered all kinds of words that I'd never heard before. Then, he started laughing and crying. The tunnel was too narrow for him, but we went to chipping and digging so fast, I was sweating for him. Chunks of mud and rock fell down the tunnel, but we didn't care. We'd done it.

I was used to having all the Unders' eyes on me when I told a story. Usually, the words flowed out of me like breath. This was different. Everything I wanted to say about the tunnel and our escaping got stuck in my throat.

Beside me, Romi whispered, "Go on. They're waiting."

I'd been waiting for this moment for so long but now that it was here, I was afraid to say the words.

"Shush," Lila said to the younguns at her feet. They were getting impatient. A few diggers yawned.

"Ama's got news," Romi said. She hardly ever spoke up like that. Hearing her voice gave me strength to find my own.

"It's time to do what Jacob always wanted us to. It's time to leave the Underland. We got a way out." Everyone stared at me like bugs were wiggling out of my ears. "You might not want to believe it, but it's not safe here anymore. It's not just me who thinks so. Sari said so too."

Nearby, Kibo bristled. "I'm not going just because a City person says I should. She doesn't know. Old Father is who I'm gonna listen to. And he wants us to stay."

I was afraid to look at the other Unders' faces. What if no one wanted to follow us to the outside? But Kibo's words were met with silence. No one jumped to join him.

"What she's saying is true. It's time for us to leave." Noah came out of the darkness and stood beside me. Dirt was streaked across his face. It was in his hair and on his tunic. While I'd been talking to the Unders, he'd been working on making the tunnel wider.

"How?" A chorus of voices rose up. "How are we gonna get out?"

"Before Jacob got taken, he and I had been digging a way out. Almost every sleep time since I was about this big." I held my hand to chest height. "Old Father never grumbled about it. Not once." I shot Kibo a look and scanned the faces of the Unders around me. They were hanging on my every word, like when I told a story. Maybe it should have scared me, but it didn't. The air was as still as that moment just before a cave-in. "I knew we were close to breaking through, but when he got taken, I lost hope. I thought, 'Well, alright, Ama, I guess that's the end of thinking about seeing the outside. Of being in the light.' But then I thought, why should I give up? I've been working on this tunnel for so long. So, I started digging. And Noah helped. Noah, who never wanted any part of escaping because he thought it was impossible."

I looked to Noah, standing beside me. He was pressing his lips together hard, like he was trying to keep all kinds of things from spilling out. "I broke through. I found us a way out." For a moment, no one moved, then everyone started speaking at once.

Finally, Noah put up his hands and waited till it was quiet. "We have a way out. We have to take it." He waved the lightstick around so it reached everyone, even the younguns like Luken who hung at the back with Lila. "It's because of Ama we got this far at all. Listen to her. She's got a plan." Hearing Noah's voice made me stand taller. It was like he'd been half-dead down here and was finally coming alive.

I met Kibo's gaze. I knew what he thought, his worries about leaving. Even though no one had spoken up, I was sure he wasn't the only one who felt that way. "It's gonna be scary outside. I know that. But it's scary staying in the Underland too. Never knowing who Krux's eyes are gonna fall on." I reached out a hand to Romi, who was beside me like always. "What we do down here is surviving, not living. We got a chance to go and I think we should take it."

Kibo put up his hand as soon as I was done talking. "I'm not trying to tell anyone what they should or shouldn't do," Kibo said. He kept his voice quiet, so we had lean in to hear him. "Ama knows my feelings. Old Father needs us down here. Big Mother too. Leaving is wrong. This is where we belong. Who we are is Underlanders. It's who we've always been."

There was a murmur of agreement from some of the older diggers. "We don't have time to argue. Whoever wants to leave, move to that side of the pit," said Noah.

I held my breath. There was talking and shuffling. Romi was the first to go to the Leaving side. Then others joined her. The younguns looked confused. Lila crouched down and explained to them and they all followed her to the Leaving side too. Pretty soon, the crowd on the Leaving side had stretched all the way to the middle of the pit. There was just a few of Unders waiting on the Stay side. Kibo was one of them. Our whole lives, we'd been together. Not in the same way as Romi and me, but I hated thinking about Kibo being all alone in the Underland.

"I'm staying too," Abel said. A couple of other diggers crossed over. There were still a lot more of us Unders leaving than staying. I winced thinking about what it would be like down here with so few people. It'd be lonely and cold. How would they ever meet the quota of brine with such a small team?

But they'd have Old Father and Big Mother. The thought of never rubbing the smooth bump around her middle made my heart sad. Without Big Mother, there'd be no more mothers, which meant no more younguns. "The mothers!" I shouted. I'd forgotten all about them.

There was a moment of stunned silence. "I know where they are," I said. "I can get them."

Noah's eyes widened in shock. "How do you—?"

"Don't ask," I replied, shaking my head at him.

"What about the fathers? Will Old Father let them go?" one of the younguns asked.

I hesitated. Had the mothers been telling the truth?

Noah frowned and answered for me. "There haven't been fathers for a long time."

"But there's younguns," Lila gave a laugh like she knew more than we did. "Course there's gotta be fathers!"

"I'm telling you, there are no fathers!" Noah's voice rose and the little ones cowered back into the shadows. We all stayed quiet till we knew his outburst was over. "Krux has his ways. His job is to make sure there's diggers and mules, more girls than boys so the population stays steady. Fathers are a danger to him. He doesn't send them to Old Father. He kills them."

The truth hung in the air. Kibo's back straightened. "All of them?"

Noah nodded. "Every one." It didn't make me feel better, but the mothers had been telling the truth.

Lila's jaw dropped. "How long have you known this?"

Noah couldn't look at her. "Too long," he said quietly. "I couldn't tell that to children." We all looked at Noah like we were seeing him for the first time. "Ama, you go to the mothers and tell them what we're doing. They need to have the choice to leave too." A whole lot of heads nodded at that. "Get anything you're taking with you and strap it to your back."

"The climb is hard. Tight too. We're gonna have to help each other," I added, grinning at everyone. "But we're used to doing that."

The pit came alive. It was like lifting a rock and finding a bunch of bugs wiggling all over. "Sounds like you were right about the fathers," Kibo said, finding me as I was rolling up a blanket for Luken.

I nodded. "I know you think Old Father wants us to stay, but we had to dig through Old Father to get to the outside. If he didn't want that tunnel to work, he could have crushed it."

"I hope you're right, Ama. A whole lot of Unders are counting on you now."

A shiver of worry crept up my spine. If things went wrong, it'd be my fault because I was the leader.

We were so busy talking about leaving and then scurrying around, no one noticed anyone lurking in the shadows. "What's going on?"

I knew Krux's voice anywhere. We all did.

I froze where I was, so did everyone else. Even the Unders working the big light stopped pedaling. The light slowly died, so it was just a few headlamps shining on Krux and then those went off too. He pulled a lightstick out of his belt and held it up. "Noah?" There was no mistaking the zapper at his belt.

I shrank back against the wall, my breath caught in my throat. If Krux had heard, our plan was ruined. He wasn't going to let us go. I looked at all the Unders. Krux was one person, and we were lots. "I'm here," Noah said. He stepped forward so he was facing Krux.

"Why aren't the Unders digging?" he asked.

"They're going now," Noah said. He glared at Krux like he was a piece of rock that needed to be split.

"Where?" Krux asked, suspiciously. He waved the lightstick around. Abel moved his sleeping mat behind his back to keep it out of sight. A few younguns hid behind Lila's legs.

"To dig," Noah answered. "Where else would they be going?"

Krux's eyes roamed around the pit and a slow smile spread across his face. "I don't know. You tell me." He started walking slowly along the row of Unders who stood behind Noah. He stopped when he got to Romi.

She hunched her shoulders, looking as small and weak as possible, but it didn't fool him. He stuck his lightstick right in her face. The way his eyes ran over her body, lingering in some spots made puke rise in my throat.

"Get away from her!" I yelled. I couldn't help myself. I ran at him, but Noah grabbed me before I got close enough to hurt him. "I'll rip your eyes out!" I shouted, writhing and clawing my way out of Noah's grip.

"Will you?" he said calmly. "I don't think so." He pulled the zapper out of his belt and held it in front of him. I shrank back, the fight leaking out of me. If he sent a jolt through me, I'd be too weak to climb out of the escape tunnel.

"Leave him, Ama. You know where he's taking Romi," Noah whispered. My breath came in bursts. I caught his meaning. If he took her, I'd be able to get her back.

Romi looked at me. She put on a brave face and nodded but I saw her chin quivering.

No one said anything. All the Unders were watching, waiting to see what I did.

"Everyone, get to the tunnels!" Noah said. "Move!" His voice shook with rage.

When the rumble started, I wondered if it was because of Noah's voice. Had his yell triggered Old Father? Bits of sand and gravel fell from the ceiling of the pit.

Krux turned around, looking up. This wasn't like a tremor in the tunnels. This one felt different. Like the whole world was cracking open. I just had time to yell, "Cave-in!" before a chunk of rock landed an arm's length away and exploded. Smaller shards flew at me. I crouched down and ran to the nearest wall, covering my head with my arms. The shaking was all around me. The ground, the ceiling, and the walls. The pit shuddered.

I squeezed my elbows to my ears and shut my eyes tight.

Our whole world was falling down.

When the shaking finally stopped, I didn't want to open my eyes. I was afraid of what I'd find. But I needed to know where Romi was. I lifted my head up and looked around. Dust billowed up and hung in the air. I coughed, gasping for air. "Romi!" I shouted.

"Here!" She called back. Other voices shouted out names. Lila called out to all her younguns. The diggers called to their mules.

"Ama?" Kibo shouted.

"I'm here," I said and turned to find him. I waved the dust away from my face. Piles of rubble sat all over the pit. Dazed younguns stumbled through. Luken came towards me, bloodied from a cut on his head. His little body, all beaten and bruised, had already lived through more pain than a youngun should.

Behind Kibo, where Big Mother had hung, was a gaping hole. I scrambled across the pit, screaming *No, no, no* in my head.

Old Father and Big Mother were like me and Romi: two halves of the same thing. They worked together to keep the Underland balanced. But when I saw what Old Father had done— taken the thing that us Unders loved the most—I realized they'd never been working together. It had always been a battle, a back and forth. One gave and the other took.

Big Mother was gone, fallen and broken. Old Father had won.

Wails went up as people saw Big Mother lying on the ground in pieces. I bent down to pick up a piece of Big Mother and that was when I saw that someone was pinned under her.

It was Krux. His eyes were open, staring at the spot where Big Mother had been. A huge chunk of her had landed on his chest and probably crushed his lungs to bits. "What is it?" Romi asked coming to stand beside me.

I pointed, hardly believing it was real.

All the Unders nearby came over to see for themselves. Lila cradled a piece of Big Mother against her chest.

"Ama," Romi whispered. "Old Father's so angry, he took Big Mother from us."

I shook my head. "I don't know about that. Maybe it wasn't Old Father's doing. Maybe Big Mother did what she had to do to save us," I said. She'd sacrificed herself to protect us.

"What are we going to do with him?" Kibo asked.

Luken looked at me. "Are we going to chant his name?" he asked.

"We only chant for our people. Krux wasn't one of us," I said to Luken. I gripped Romi's hand in mine.

Noah stared at Krux's body a long time. "I wish he were still alive, only so he'd know we got free of this place," Noah murmured.

It really was time to go now. Krux was gone and so was Big Mother. There was nothing to stop us from leaving the Underland. I walked towards the pool first but when I got to the cranny that hid the escape tunnel, I froze. Huge boulders stared back at me. Our chance of getting out of the Underland had come crashing down in a landslide of rock, dirt, and grit.

"Old Father," Kibo whispered when he saw.

"No," I said. "No, no, no!"

I couldn't believe it. All that work—gone.

"I warned you," Kibo murmured. "Old Father wouldn't like it."

I buried my face in Noah's shoulder and wept. Kibo's words echoed in my head as loud as the cave-in.

"Shh," Noah whispered, stroking my head. "Shh."

My chest shook with sobs. "How could Old Father do this?" I cried. Why did he let me see the light if he was only going to take it away?

Sari

"Who are you?" I called out.

The figure stepped forward through the dusty haze and I found myself face to face with Kaia.

My heart leapt to my throat, but no words came. How many times had I wished for Kaia to return? Dreamed that it would come true. But now it was happening, and all I could do was stare at her. It was Kaia, but she was completely different. There was a wildness to her, it was on her face, a confidence I didn't remember. Over her shoulders, she wore a cape, at her waist on one side, the blade of an axe, and on the other side, a knife.

"You're alive." My voice didn't sound like my own.

She blinked at us with shock and relief. "Sari. Mae!" Her eyes flickered to me, then back to Mae. Kaia reached out, grabbing Mae's hands in hers. "I thought you were balanced. I never would have left if I'd known—"

"Oh, Kaia, I know." Mae touched Kaia's cheek as if she couldn't believe she was real. "But you should have stayed away. You shouldn't have come back."

Kaia shook her head. "I had to. Lev told me what Tar had done." She spoke to both of us. "To all of us. He found me outside. He was sick with an infection, but he's getting better. Jacob had medicine—"

"Jacob?" I interrupted her. "He's with you?" All the pieces were starting to fit together.

Kaia frowned, puzzled. "Yes. How do you know who he is?"

My head was spinning. I tucked the knife back into my satchel. "There's too much to explain," I said. I didn't even know where to begin. "You need to get out of here," I said.

"What about Sy?" Kaia asked. "Is he still alive?"

Mae and I shook our heads. Kaia cursed under her breath.

A faint vibration shook the corridor. Dust trickled down from the ceiling. I looked up anxiously. Voices came from the direction of the Underland entrance. "Get to the surface! Take the Councillors to safety!"

"What is going on?" Kaia asked. "The shaking—"

"The City isn't stable. There are tunnels underground. Mika warned the Council, but they won't listen. It's going to collapse."

"What's going to collapse? The tunnel?" Kaia asked.

I shook my head. "The City."

Kaia's eyes grew wide.

"It gets worse," I said. "The people Jacob lived with—"

"I know about the Underlanders," Kaia interrupted. "Jacob explained everything. We're here to free them and to get Mae." With all my heart, I wanted her to add, 'And you.' But she didn't, and I couldn't blame her. I'd made a choice that had cost her everything. A tremor began, a long, low rumble that warned of worse to come. Kaia ducked and pulled Mae closer to her when a piece of ceiling fell and landed at her feet. Her face creased with worry. "It's really going to collapse?" she asked.

I nodded. There was another tremor.

"You can't stay here!" Kaia whispered. "Please come with me. The outside isn't what you think, neither are the Prims."

Part of me wanted to go with her. To leave the City and its troubles behind. But Mika's last message ran through my head. *The baby.* She needed me. So did Ren. He was still trapped somewhere down here. "I can't," I said. "Not yet." I wanted to tell her I was sorry. That I'd failed her when she needed me the most. That I'd saved Mae because I knew that was what she would have wanted. And I wanted to share silly stuff too—that I'd met someone I really liked. That Mika and I were spending time together and that she was pregnant. "There's so much I want to tell you." My voice broke.

"Me too," she said. "You have no idea."

"I wish I'd never been matched with Lev," I blurted. "I never meant to hurt you."

Kaia gave me a long look. "I've learned things about the City. It's—it's not what you think it is. Come with me."

As much as I cared about Kaia, I knew I couldn't leave. "I can't. People are depending on me." A flicker of surprise crossed her face. Kaia wasn't the only one who had changed.

There were shouts from another corridor. She gave me a final, pleading look, but I held firm and shook my head. "Be careful," she said to me.

"You too." Those were the last words we said to each other before she led Mae away.

As I strode towards the City entrance, all I could do was hope I'd made the right choice.

Ama

All the fight I'd had in me leaked out. I was just too tired. I'd been digging and hoping for so long, but none of it mattered. Old Father didn't want us to go, so we weren't going. Kibo was right. We belonged here. Dead or alive, we were Old Father's. "There's no way out now."

Noah's voice was flat like the pool. "We could dig through it again." But no one believed he meant it.

Why Old Father? Why do you want us here so bad? I looked at Lila, at the heartbreak on her face as she picked up what was left of Big Mother.

Hoping hadn't worked.

Neither had digging.

A rage like I'd never felt before exploded out of me. I balled up my fists and took a deep breath. "Old Father!" I screamed at the top of my lungs. "I hate you! You hear me? I hate you!"

Every Under turned to look at me. The ones who were crying, stopped.

The ground didn't shake. It didn't even tremble. Where was Old Father now?

And then, a deep voice echoed in the pit. It was familiar. I'd heard it in my dreams a hundred times. "Hello?"

"It's Jacob!" Kibo shouted.

It couldn't be.

"Old Father sent him back, Ama!"

I didn't want to look because I didn't want it to be wrong. I didn't want a City person to be marching behind him with a zapper to his back. Another trick by Old Father. Mutterings of his name were like shivers up and down my spine. I looked up at Noah and when I saw his expression, I knew it wasn't a trick. Jacob had come back.

Sari

Citizens raced along the walkways, running for their dwellings. I moved quickly, intent on getting to Mika. As I got closer to her dwelling, I saw a Citizen jump into the stream. It was usually deep, but today the water only came to his knees. He had two gourds with him and after he'd filled them, he tossed them up and two more were thrown down to him. "He's stealing the water!" someone on a balcony shouted.

There were more hollers for him to stop and calls to the overseers to help. None of them came. They were all standing in front of the dome, staring outside.

"What's going on?" I asked an older Citizen. She was crouched in the doorway of a dwelling.

"The Prims are here." Her eyes widened at the word.

"And they cut off the water?"

"They're trying to get inside. They want the City for themselves!"

"Why aren't the overseers doing anything?" I asked.

The female shrugged. "What can they do? The Council is in hiding."

It was worse than I thought. The messages on my newsfeed were garbled. Too much information was coming in at once. If the Council was in hiding, who was in charge of the overseers? I rushed up to Mika's dwelling. "Mika!" I called as I burst in. She was sitting on the floor and Dex was lying behind her. She didn't move. "Mika?"

Mika whimpered, her eyes round and terrified. "What is it?" I looked to the left and saw Ren. Relief flooded through me. "You escaped!"

But his face didn't show any joy. That was when I realized the taser in his hand was pointed at me.

"I'm sorry," Mika cried. "He made me send the message. To you and Dex."

I still didn't understand. "What's going on?"

"Shut the door," he said.

I did as he said, but a body-numbing chill started in my stomach and spread.

"He tasered Dex!" Mika said.

"Did he hurt you?" I asked. Mika shook her head, but now I could see her hands were tied behind her back. "You're a traitor," I whispered to him.

Ren smirked. "A traitor to the traitors. Yes, I am. I'm also the offspring of a Councillor. Putting an end to the CORE has secured me a spot on the Council." He glared at me triumphant.

"I trusted you," I said through clenched teeth. A flush of shame rose up my neck. How could I have been so foolish? The first person to show interest and I fell for him like an idiot. He knew the truth about the Underland, our plan to help free Ama and her people. I looked at Mika, and Dex lying behind her. "I thought you wanted to save the City."

"The CORE can't save the City. You can't even protect yourselves," he nodded his head at Mika and Dex. "Your plan won't keep the City safe; it will end it. Citizens don't want to know where their energy comes from. All that matters is that it keeps coming." He scoffed. "You care more about the Underlanders than your own people."

"This isn't just about protecting the Underlanders. The tremors affect everyone. The dome could collapse. You *know* that!"

"The Council has a plan."

Despite the taser pointed in my direction, I laughed. "The Council has known about this for months and they've done nothing!" Tar and the others were more concerned with holding power than saving the City.

"It might be too late!" Mika said.

I hadn't realized until that moment how dangerous the Council really was. It was one thing not to know the truth, it was another to hide it. And Ren! He was so desperate to be a Councillor, he was willing to go along with them.

There was a flicker of doubt on Ren's face.

"You know we're right, Ren. Getting rid of us won't change the truth. Not just about the danger facing the City, but about who's leading us." I met his eyes and held them for a long moment. "Let Mika go."

"I can't," he said. "I made my choice." He grabbed my arm and held the taser to my neck. Ren's breath was hot in my ear.

"Don't hurt her!" Mika cried out. Her hands were tied behind her back, but she struggled to her feet, lunging at Ren. She misjudged the distance and lost her balance. There was a sickening gasp as she landed hard on her stomach.

"Mika!" I screamed and wrenched myself from Ren's grip, falling to the ground beside her.

"Do something," she murmured. Her face was set with grim determination. I didn't give myself time to think. If I was going to save us, I had to do it now. I reached into my satchel. My hand closed around the handle of the knife.

"Get up!" Ren yelled as he yanked on my arm. I spun around

and jammed the knife into his side. It took more strength than I imagined, and I fell away breathing hard. My whole body shook because of what I'd just done.

Ren looked at me in shock. A slow bloom of blood spread across his tunic. He stumbled backward and into the wall, clutching his side. The taser clattered to the floor. The sound echoed against the walls. No one moved.

There was a noise at the entrance. The door opened, but I was afraid to look. My breath came in jagged gasps. If it was overseers, they'd take me to a cell. There'd be no point to going before the Council. I was guilty and I'd be sent to the Underland to be balanced.

"Mika! Dex!" Avi's voice cut through the sounds of rising panic outside. "Sari? What the—" He took in the scene in front of him, his eyes landing on Ren, slumped against the wall, the hilt of the knife sticking out of his side.

"What happened?" he asked and rushed to Ren. He looked up at me with disbelief.

I bent down, decisive now about what I had to do. Avi wasn't an overseer. He didn't hold sway with the Council; he wasn't even part of the CORE anymore. If I was smart, I could use him to get me out of this mess. When Avi looked up again, it wasn't at me, it was straight into the barrel of Ren's taser.

Ama

"It's really you!" I said, still not believing my eyes. He looked different. His skin colour was darker and his long, shaggy hair and beard had been trimmed. He didn't look like a City person, or like an Under.

"Jacob." The word came out of Noah like a sigh and a sob. He grabbed him and they held on to each other for a long time.

Jacob looked around the pit. He took in the piles of rubble and the hole in the ceiling where Big Mother had hung since forever. He didn't look sad though, his eyes were bright. I hated to tell him that there was no way out. He'd come back and now he was gonna be trapped again. "There was a cave-in," I started. "The escape tunnel is gone." I hung my head as I said it, like it was my fault. Maybe it was. Maybe Kibo was right and Old Father didn't want us to leave.

"Anyone hurt?" Jacob asked. I waited for his eyes to dim, but they didn't. They kept shining like the big light was inside of him.

"Krux. Big Mother killed him." It was little Luken who spoke.

It was Jacob's turn to stare at us in disbelief.

"It's true," Noah said and pointed. "Crushed him."

Jacob's mouth twisted with disappointment. "Too quick an end for him," he muttered to Noah.

"How'd you get here?" Kibo said stepping forward. "We thought you were with the Fathers."

Jacob grinned. "Old Father sent me back. Can you believe it? He didn't want you Unders living in the dark anymore. He's got a new home for you."

"A new home?" Luken repeated.

Jacob put a finger to his lips. "It's a secret. You need to follow me and be very quiet."

Instead of doing what Jacob said, the Unders looked at me. Me, standing by myself with a throat sore from yelling. Jacob frowned. "Ama?"

"We've been let down so many times," I said shaking my head. "Tell us everything so we can decide for ourselves."

Jacob gave me a long look, the kind that made me stand up straighter. Then he started speaking. All us Unders crowded closer to listen. "When Krux took me, he sent me outside with another City person. We were supposed to find someone who'd escaped. Her name was Kaia and she was my youngun from many years ago." He waited till the murmurs of surprise died down. "When I found her, she didn't want to come back, and I didn't blame her. We went to the Mountain and found the Prims. They thought I'd been dead all this time." Jacob looked at Noah, whose chin was trembling. Jacob's voice cracked with emotion when he started talking again. "Since I've been away, all I've thought about was coming back to you. The Prims are outside waiting. I snuck back into the City through a tunnel and that's the same way we're leaving."

No one moved.

"You can have a new life outside. A real life. No more digging. No more worrying about a cave-in. The Prims are waiting for you."

I closed my eyes and took a deep breath. I breathed in all the stories that I'd told for all the years we'd been down here. If we were going, I was taking them with me. "Ama? What are we gonna do?" Romi looked at me with her trusting eyes. We'd always been two halves of the same. I wasn't leaving without her and she wasn't leaving without me.

"Old Father took away one choice, but he's giving us another. He sent Jacob back." The sound of breaking rock filled the pit. It echoed off the walls. I raised my eyes to the ceiling. Every Under stayed silent, waiting to see if Old Father agreed. Nothing else happened.

"Old Father's telling us to go," I said. "He's not mad. He's making sure we understand: our time down here is done." I gave Kibo a long look.

"I don't know why I ever bother arguing with you," he muttered. "You always get your way."

It was time to go.

Kibo grabbed the headlamps and lightsticks from Noah's station and handed them out, waving his to get everyone's attention.

"Get what you can carry!" Jacob shouted. "Younguns travel in the middle with Lila. Mules at the front, diggers at the back."

Jacob and Noah herded the Underlanders into a line. Some of them grabbed what little they had, a sleeping mat maybe. Or a token someone had given them. My arms were empty. I'd breathed in the stories. There was nothing else I needed.

Except Romi. I spotted her helping Lila with the younguns. Luken was clutching her hand, his eyes wide and scared. "The mothers," Romi whispered as she walked past me and into the passage. "You have to get them out."

Amidst everything, I'd forgotten about them again. I looked back at the line of Unders snaking down the corridor. We weren't hard to miss. How long until a City person found us?

Luken grabbed my hand and held it tightly, yanking me with him. "Come!" he begged. "Old Father is angry. He hurt Big Mother." In his other hand was a shard of Big Mother.

I looked at Romi. I had to get to the mothers and join the rest of the group. "That wasn't Old Father's fault. He wanted Big Mother to be free, like us. Now she can go wherever she wants, Luken. And so can we. Stay close to Romi," I pulled my hand out of his grip. "I'll be back soon."

"Ama!" I heard Jacob call to me as I raced past the line of Unders. Without looking back, I took the turn that would lead me to the mothers. I wasn't being careful as I raced down the passage. The door to the mothers' cell was the first one with a bar blocking it. My headlamp glowed as energy coursed through me. I just had to find it and free them, then I could go back to my Unders. To Jacob and Luken and Romi.

"Sela! Valla!" I shouted and banged on the door. I didn't care who heard me. I needed to get them out. There was a shuffle on the other side of the door.

"Who is it?"

I heaved the bar and swung the door open, and all five of them stared at me. "We're leaving. The pit is collapsing. We have a way out."

I guess if someone had come to me with the same words, I'd have done what the mothers did. Which was nothing.

"We can't leave. Look at us." Olga waved her hands at their bellies.

Valla shook her head. "My baby's coming soon. Where will we go?"

"Outside. Jacob is taking us. His people are here."

"You said Jacob was gone. He's back now?"

They were confused, but I got impatient and stamped my foot. What if the Unders left without me? What if I never found my way out and was stuck here? "It doesn't matter! Just follow me."

They dug their heels in. "No. We have babies to worry about. What if Krux finds out?"

"There was a cave-in in the pit. Krux is dead and Big Mother is shattered."

All of them gasped. Without Big Mother, there was no one to protect them. "She wants us to go," I said, trying to make them understand.

"Go where?" Sela asked.

"The Mountain."

They gaped at me and looked at each other.

"Please," I begged. "We have to go *now*. The younguns are waiting for you."

There were more gasps. It hadn't occurred to them that they could be together outside. "Our children!"

"Yes!" I shouted triumphantly. "You can be with your children. If you follow me. We can all be together."

Another tremor shook the ground. I braced myself against the doorway. All the mothers looked at each other. They knew I was right; I could see it on their faces. When the shaking stopped, Olga held out her arm to Valla, who heaved her to standing.

"Show us the way," Olga said. The others nodded.

I breathed a sigh of relief and went first into the corridor. The five of them followed, helping each other. I didn't know who to thank for making them listen: Big Mother or Old Father. So I thanked them both as the mothers followed me into the tunnel.

"How far is it?" Olga asked. She was slow, her steps lumbering. They weren't used to moving after living so long in that little room. She pressed her lips together like everything was hurting. Sela held her hand, pulling her forward.

Where was Jacob? I sniffed the air, but it was thick with the strong smell of the mothers. Prickles of worry ran up my spine. *What if we were lost?*

I pushed my doubts away and kept moving. A little further up, I heard something. I raised a hand to stop the mothers. We stayed where we were until I was sure I knew who it was. The walk and the stoop of the shoulders belonged to Jacob. He was leading the Unders through the corridor. Even with all of them behind him, there was still barely a sound. Their feet were just whispers on the ground.

Jacob swung his lightstick so it landed on me, and then the mothers. He put his finger to his lips, a signal to keep quiet. The big reunion would wait until later. I searched the line of people. There was only one person I needed to see. When my eyes found her, I let out the breath I didn't know I was holding.

We were so close. *Please let us go,* I prayed to Old Father and Big Mother. All I could do was hope one of them was listening.

Sari

Avi stood and held up his hands. "I'm on your side, Sari." Was he telling the truth? I'd fallen for Ren's lies and it had almost cost us everything. "You wanted out." I held the taser tightly, keeping it aimed at his chest. "I can't trust you." Avi didn't move any closer. From outside the dwelling, there was shouting. Something was going on. "The images have gone out," he said. I lowered the taser slightly. "They'll be on your newsfeed in a second."

In my ear, the voice said, "Underland secrets revealed! The City is in danger. Not from Prims, but from its own Council. Underground tremors threaten the foundation of the dome." If I didn't have a taser in my hands, I would have pulled up my hologram to see the images, which was what other Citizens must have been doing. The uproar was deafening.

"The Council's time is done," he said. "They can't come back from this. The Citizens are going to see who they really are."

Ren groaned. The pool of blood on the floor was spreading. "He needs help," Avi said. He looked to Mika. "Are you okay? Is Dex?"

Mika nodded. She rolled over and tried to sit up. As I went to untie her hands, Avi sent a message asking for medical help. "How did you know I was here?" I asked Avi.

"I didn't. It was Ren I was tracking."

I got a flash of guilt at the way I'd written Avi off as weak-willed. "Why did you suspect him?"

"My intel on him didn't add up. Why would the offspring of a Councillor want to be part of the CORE? I took a look at his personality profile. He ranked high for—"

"Moral ambiguity," I said with a sigh.

Avi nodded. "Yours did too," he said ruefully, "but your

reasons made sense. Ren's didn't. We started to wonder if he was working against us."

"We?"

"Dex and I."

"Dex?" Mika had crawled over to Dex and was stroking his brow, but at this revelation, her head snapped up.

"He never told me."

"The argument a few nights ago was staged. A fake to throw Ren off. We needed him to think I'd bailed on the plan. When you and he went into the Underland, his pulse point wasn't scrambled. We were able to track his movement. Turned out, he and Krux orchestrated his disappearance. As soon as he was sure you'd continued to the Underland, he came back here. What he didn't count on was the Prim attack."

I glanced at Ren. His eyes were closed. It looked like he was concentrating on each breath. It was wrong of me, but I didn't feel guilty for what I'd done. I didn't want him to be in pain, but he would have sent Mika, Dex and me to an Underland cell for doing what we knew was right.

"What happens now?"

"Some friends are on their way."

"Friends?" I asked.

"We aren't the only CORE group in the City," Avi said. "There are others. We stay separate to protect ourselves. The overseers guarding the Council are CORE. So are most of the Citizens who work in Communications."

Dex nodded. As we spoke, two people came to the door. One I recognized as the fruit seller from the market. The other was the chatty overseer who had distracted Ren. "My friends, Max and Yulim," he said. Yulim had a bag of medical supplies with her. She went to Ren and inspected his wound. "It's bad, but not deadly," she said. I'll admit, I felt some relief hearing that.

"You handled yourself well," Avi said. "You're more resourceful than I expected."

Avi's eyes glowed with admiration. The shiftiness I'd been wary of at our earlier meetings had been directed at Ren, not me. "Max and Yulim have things under control here," Avi said. "I want to know what's going on outside."

I looked to Mika. "Go," she said. "As soon as Dex is up to it, we'll follow."

I went with Avi to the landing between the third and fourth floors. We had a good view of the City, but also of what lay beyond the dome. Citizens were uneasy. They wanted their voices heard but shouted out to no one in particular. "Where's the Council?" someone called out.

"In hiding! Too scared to face us!"

The overseers were still crowded around the perimeter of the dome watching the Prims. From where we stood, I could see why the stream had dried up. The Prims had dammed it from the outside. A lake was growing on the other side of the dome.

"Once the water is gone, we're at their mercy."

"You sound impressed," I said looking at Avi.

"It's a clever plan," Avi said. "Working together to cut down the trees and float them down the stream, then to plan how to assemble the dam. I don't think they're as backwards as the Council wants us to believe."

Beyond the lake, a camp had been set up. Fabric was tied across logs stuck into the ground to provide wind and sun protection. Mika arrived with Dex, joining us on the landing. "What are you looking at?" she asked. Dex was moving slowly, leaning against Mika. Avi explained and when he was done, Mika shook her head, frowning.

"What is it?" I asked. "Is it the baby?

"No, it's not that. It's the way the Prims dammed the stream. Look at the size of the lake they created. The bedrock underneath is already unstable, riddled with tunnels. The weight of the water could make it collapse. The dome would go with it." As if to prove Mika's point, the dome creaked. It was a different sound than when the wind blew hard and the solar panels undulated. This was a grinding noise coming from the skeletal frame of the dome. An eerie quiet settled over the City.

"What's the worst-case scenario?" Dex asked.

Mika thought carefully. "Worst case? The ground under the lake buckles. The Underland will collapse and the dome with it." She looked at each of us. "It could be catastrophic."

"Not just for us," I said with a sigh. "What about the Underlanders?" I thought of Ama and how desperate she'd been for help. "They wouldn't be able to escape."

"They'd drown," Avi said, wincing.

"What if the Prims undam it?" Dex asked.

"If the water is suddenly released, we'll have the same problem. It'll rush into the City with too much force. The best thing would be to dig a trench and divert it." As Mika spoke, the dome's creaks grew louder. It sounded like it was begging for help. The sound brought more Citizens to their balconies. The overseers looked to each other. They were used to following orders, not thinking for themselves.

I gulped because the reality of the situation was dawning on me. Without a Council we could trust, it was up to us to come up with a plan. Time was running out. If we wanted to save the City, we were going to have to do it ourselves.

Ama

I fell in line behind Jacob, with Romi beside me. He turned down a tunnel that branched off the one that had led out of the pit. The slope of the corridor rose gradually. We kept walking, the whole group of us silently marching until he got to a spot where a barely visible rectangle had been cut out of the wall. If Jacob hadn't stopped at it, I'd have never known it was there.

"Have you always known about this?" I asked him. All the time we'd been digging, we could've just snuck out!

"A City person told me."

"You're trusting City people?"

"I'm trusting this one," Jacob said. "It's safe, Ama. I promise."

When he pushed on it, the sound was rock grinding against rock.

"At the end of the secret tunnel is the outside." He waved me and Romi through first. *Please Big Mother*, I thought, *watch over us.* I clutched Romi's hand. Our headlamps lit up the walls. The tunnel was long, just as long as our escape tunnel out of the pit had been. It felt like forever when we finally saw something up ahead.

"Ama! Look!" Romi pointed to a patch of light. "Do you think that's the end?" We hurried up our steps. The Unders behind us saw it too.

"It's the sun!" I said. "Just like Jacob talked about. It's like our big light, only different." We raced ahead, running until we were right in front of it. When I stretched out my hand, it wasn't just bright, it was warm too. A man's head peered down the hole.

"They're here!" his voice boomed. "You gotta climb out," he said. "Grab the ladder."

Ladder. It was the thing hanging down in front of me. I looked at it, unsure. This was it. Once we left this tunnel, there was no going back.

Romi leaned down so her lips were beside my ear. "You can do it," she whispered.

"Put your feet on that bottom rung," the Prim told me, "and your hands up higher. There you go," he said when I got it right. "Now climb up, move your hand first and then your foot."

"It's like crawling," I said, looking at the line of Unders behind me, watching.

A few more rungs of the ladder and the man at the top reached his hands down to me. He grabbed me under the arms and hauled me through the opening. The burst of air hit me. It was dry and hot and burned my throat. I gulped and looked around. The wind bit at my skin. I stumbled away from the hole I'd crawled out of. Bits of grit flew in my face. The brightness stung my eyes, but I didn't want to close them. I didn't want to lose one moment of seeing the outside. There was the sky. It stretched all around, touching land and the Mountain in the distance. It rose up like the A in Ama, just like Jacob had shown me.

"Oh, Big Mother," I breathed. Was she seeing what I saw?

Next Romi climbed out and then Luken. Kibo came next. They all stood beside me in stunned silence. "It's loud," Luken said and covered his ears. He was right. Big white sticks stuck out of the ground. Things spun on the end. Watching them made me dizzy. "So this is outside," he said. He looked around.

"Big Mother's here," I said. "I can feel her." The sun's warmth was Big Mother smiling on us.

"Old Father too," Kibo said. He put a hand to his chest. "I can feel him right here."

"Is he angry?" Luken asked.

Kibo thought on the question. "I don't think so." He grinned at Luken. "I think maybe he needed us to help him get free, same as we needed him."

More Unders climbed out of the hole, and when Sela appeared,

Kibo's face brightened. I knew that look. It was the same one I got on my face around Romi.

Another Prim came towards us. A woman with a long braid. "I'm Mara," she said. "You made it." When she smiled at me, I wanted to say something, but my mouth wouldn't work right. No words came out, even though my head was full of them.

"Come," she said. "We need to get you past the wind turbines and into the shade. You'll be safe there." I looked back at all the Unders coming up from the ground. And then, I looked at the dome.

Inside, City people crowded around watching us. Their mouths hung open in o's of surprise. What would I have done if I suddenly learned there'd been a whole group of people living in an even darker dark below us Unders?

I looked at the City people and searched for Sari. And then, I saw her. She wasn't standing with the other City people; she was above them on a platform. I didn't know if she could see me, but I wanted to yell to her: We did it! Us Unders were free.

Sari

"Sari!" Mika gasped. She was pointing outside. "Look!" The line of Underlanders stumbled from an opening in the ground. A few stood in a group. They looked so small with their spindly limbs. How they'd eked out an existence in the dark of the Underland was a mystery. One of them turned towards the City, searching for something. She had a head of sparse curls. *Ama*. I breathed a sigh of relief. "Jacob," I murmured. He'd gone back to free them, just like Kaia had said. Had she made it out with Mae?

More and more Citizens emerged from their dwellings. Balconies on higher stories were crowded with neighbours all curious about what was going on outside.

"It's just like on our newsfeed," someone said. "Those are the people from the Underland."

I let the comment echo in my head. No one would have known about the Underlanders if it hadn't been for us. "Energy level low," a voice said in my ear. I glanced at my pulse point. After not visiting the gymnasium in so long, I wouldn't have enough to last the day. If it reached zero, an overseer would pay me a visit. Before, the threat of drawing the attention of an overseer was enough to make me rush to the gymnasium. But now, it was laughable. We had bigger problems. I pressed my thumb against my finger, feeling for the little chip that lay under my skin.

"It's time to make ourselves visible," I said. "All the CORE have to show themselves. We have to show the Council and the Citizens that there is another way. Fear can't control us. We need to be the leaders. We need to talk to the Prims."

Mika's hands went to her stomach. Dex shook his head. "That's not a good idea. We're already weakened. The Prims are dangerous. We still don't know why they're here."

"I do," I said.

Mika gaped at me. "You do?"

I nodded. All three of them turned to face me. "They aren't here for us. Kaia came to get Mae. Jacob, one of the Prims who was held in the Underland came back to free the Underlanders. I promise, the Prims don't care about the City."

Avi considered what I said. He turned to Mika. "If you think digging a diversion is the only way to keep the City standing, Sari's right. We need to go outside. We need to talk to the Prims."

The dome creaked again. "How do we get out?" I asked.

"The escape hatch," Avi pointed to a flap at the top of the spiral staircase. It was how Lev and Raf had left to go after Kaia. The rope ladder they'd used to climb down was still dangling, waiting for their return. "The other entrances are sealed shut. They have been for decades."

"And if we have to evacuate? What then? Getting everyone out using the escape hatch would take days," Mika said. The furrow between her eyes deepened.

"We need to open one of the sealed entrances," Dex said.

"But we don't know where they are," Mika reminded them.

I turned to Mika and our faces lit up with the same idea at the same time. "The MAP!" I didn't worry about anyone seeing my hologram or the Mining Access Plan appear in the air in front of me. "It has all the City plans." I scrolled through the files and found the one labeled 'Egress Routes'. "This is it! It shows all of them." Knowing we weren't going to be trapped in a crumbling City gave me a burst of hope. Being outside wasn't my first choice, but if the dome fell...I shook my head and reminded myself to deal with problems one at a time.

I swiped to my contacts and sent the file to all three of them. "You'll have to figure out a way to open them and get the information to the Citizens," I said as I slipped my satchel off my shoulder and passed it to Mika.

"What are you doing?" she asked.

"One of us has to go out there. The Prims need to know what's going on. We're going to need their help."

"No!" Mika said, shaking her head.

"One of us has to. It makes sense if I go. Kaia's out there. Lev too, probably. They won't let anything happen to me." We didn't have time to argue. It was nice that she cared, and a little ironic since we'd spent most of our lives at odds with each other.

Mika still looked unsure. "You know I'm right," I said gently. "I can't do the things the three of you can, but I can do this."

"She's right," Avi said. "Someone has to go. If the Prims see Citizens pouring out of the City, they'll think they're being attacked. While Sari is outside, we can do what we need to and get the Citizens ready."

Dex nodded. "We can send out another message on the newsfeed. Citizens need to know what's happening. They've lived in the dark for too long."

Another creak from the dome made the line between Avi's eyebrows deepen. "There are other CORE members willing to help. I'll contact them." Avi spoke with such authority, I wondered how he'd scored on his personality profile. He was a leader through and through. Had it shown up in his job placement? Or was he deemed a threat and ignored? Given a job that would keep him occupied in the Underland counting joules.

"Are you sure you want to do this?" Mika asked me. She put her hands on my shoulders and made me face her.

"I'm sure," I said.

But as I went down the stairs and across the walkway to the spiral staircase, the worries flooded in. I was venturing to a place filled with dangers, to speak with the people we were taught to fear. I'd only have one chance to convince the Prims that the future of the City and the lives of its Citizens depended on their help.

Ama

At first, the light was warm. But after we'd been under the sun it started to bite, like a sharp rock pricking our skin. As much as I wanted to see *everything*, take it all in and gobble it up, my eyes wouldn't let me.

"You're hurting?" Mara asked.

I nodded. We all were, but we were too scared to say anything. "Jacob warned us it'd be hard for you after living in the dark for so long." She led us to a shelter built of sticks that leaned together and had fabric wrapped around it. All us Unders squished inside of it, safe from the sun's burning brightness.

My stomach churned with worry. What other dangers had Jacob kept hidden from us?

"Ama?" Romi's hand found mine. "I'm scared," she whispered.

I hated to say it, but I'd be lying if I didn't. "Me too."

"How long are we going to stay here?" someone asked.

"Till the sun goes down," I said. "Jacob told me the sun will sink behind the Mountain and that's called *night*. It'll be the moon's turn to light up the sky and it's not as bright. It'll be just like in the Underland and that's when we're going to start walking."

"Can you tell me a story, Ama," Luken said, snuggling up close.

"About what?" I asked giving his ear a tweak.

"About how us Unders found our way to the light."

I sighed and stared out at the Mountain. "I don't know how this story ends, Luken."

"Sure you do," Romi said, settling beside me. She gave me one of her long, quiet looks that said more than a hundred words could have.

I closed my eyes and started talking. This story wasn't coming from the air of the Underland. All the words I needed were deep inside me. "Once, there were people called Underlanders who grew tired of living the way they did. It was dangerous and the Unders didn't want to see any more of them get taken by Old Father, or Krux. So, they made a plan to escape. But what they discovered was that plans don't always work out. They had to try again and again until finally, a man named Jacob came to save them. He led the Unders to the outside where the light was harsh. But even in the hard light that made their eyes ache, they could see where they'd been and where they could go. The hope they'd carried inside of them like a little nugget of light got bigger and bigger until it was all around them. That's how us Unders stopped surviving and started living. We showed the City people that just because we lived in the dark, didn't make us dim."

Everyone sat quietly, holding on to the story, until Romi spoke. "Your story is almost perfect," she said. She'd never criticized my stories before.

"Almost?" I asked.

"It wasn't Jacob that got us out," she said. "It was you."

"Jacob's the one who knew about that other tunnel."

"That's not what I mean," she said. "Anyone could have shown us the way out. What we needed was to believe we could do it." She gave my hand a squeeze and the way she looked at me made me think I could do anything.

Sari

It was easier to unlock the hatch than I expected. All this time, anyone could have left the City if they'd wanted to.

With one heave, it flew open. I hesitated for a moment and then I lifted my head to the outside. For the first time in my life, I didn't have a dome around me. I turned my head and looked in every direction. It was huge.

The wind whipped up behind me, dirt swirled on the ground below. My eyes leaked tears, the dry air burned. I licked my lips, my mouth already gummy with dryness. Is this what it had felt like for Kaia? I coughed as the dry air ripped through my lungs. My eyes burned from the sharp glare of the sun. From the top of the dome, the valley stretched in front of me, with the newly formed lake shimmering below. Shelters for the Unders and the Prims dotted the sandy landscape.

I took a deep breath and winced. The lack of humidity would

take some getting used to. "Kaia!" I shouted, but my voice was stolen away by the wind. "Kaia!" It was too hard to yell.

A group of Prims moved closer to the dome, watching me warily. One motioned with his hands that he couldn't hear me. I'd have to go down. The panels undulated as the wind picked up. I'd never felt wind like this; it was like an invisible arm pushing me.

My heart beat quickly and I steadied my breath. Somewhere below, I hoped Kaia was watching me. I clung to that thought as I grabbed the rope ladder and began my descent.

The wind kicked up again. I held on tightly to the rope. I wasn't afraid of heights, but I'd never been suspended ten stories above the ground on the outside of the dome before either. I ignored the sting of the air in my lungs and took a deep breath.

"Sari!" Over the gusts of wind I heard Kaia's voice. "I'm here!"

I moved one foot down, carefully placing it on the next rung, and then moved my hands. Sweat dripped down my face and made my hands slippery. I was too afraid to see how much further I had to go. I was sure there were Citizens and overseers inside the City watching me, but I didn't want to think about that right now. I concentrated on one thing—how good flat ground would feel under my feet.

"Keep going!" Kaia called. "You're almost there!"

I dropped to the ground. My legs were weak and my arms trembled. "I did it!" I rasped. I was too parched to swallow.

"Sari!" Kaia fell to the ground beside me. "I can't believe it! You're actually here! You're outside!" Kaia wrapped her arms around me. It was awkward and we almost toppled over. Having her so close, breathing in her musky, sweaty odour, reminded me this wasn't a dream. "What made you change your mind?" she asked.

"Kaia," I said slowly. "I'm not here to join you. I need your help."

Her face fell. "What kind of help?"

We shared a long look. I saw her wariness and the flicker of distrust that made her pull away from me. I took a breath, but the dry air made me cough. "You need to drink." She passed me a gourd of water. I gulped it down and gave it back to her.

"Sari!"

I turned at the familiar voice. Lev shook his head in shock. "What are you doing?" Like Kaia, he'd changed a lot since he'd been gone. His hair and skin, of course—the time outside had weathered him—but something else too.

"I can't believe you're alive," I said. Kaia held out her hand and helped me to my feet.

He grunted. "Barely." He held up a walking stick. There was a haunted look in his eyes. I realized that was what was different about him. The innocence he'd had before he'd left the City was gone.

"Kaia said the outside isn't what we think." I looked to him for confirmation. Had she been telling the truth? Or was it her Prim blood that gave her an advantage. A shadow flickered across Lev's face.

"I would have died on the Mountain if Kaia hadn't found me. Even then, I only survived because of the medicine Jacob carried with him. I'm still healing." He looked to Kaia. She gave him an encouraging smile, but it was tinged with sadness. They'd been through a lot.

"Why are you here, Sari? What do you need from us?" I saw Kaia's suspicion mirrored on Lev's face.

"Tar and the Council aren't in control anymore. There's a group of us, we're the CORE. We're changing things, exposing the Council for who they really are. We have control of the communication system."

"Is that why you were in the Underland?" Kaia asked.

I nodded. "I was trying to help the Underlanders, but it looks like they didn't need me."

Lev looked at me with disbelief. "How could the Council have lost control? Why aren't the overseers doing something?"

"When the Prim Threat Level was raised to extreme, no one knew what to do. The Council went into hiding, but the overseers guarding them are with us. Then, the CORE got control of the newsfeed. The truth is out. Citizens are discovering what really went on in the Underland. A lot of the overseers who thought they needed to guard against your attack are realizing the real danger is in the City, not out here." Everything came out in a rush. As I'd been speaking, a male Prim walked over. His eyes were the same blue as Kaia's.

"Jacob," Kaia said. "This is Sari."

He tilted his head and surveyed me. "You were the one who went to the Underland. Noah told me about you." He turned to Kaia. "He said she's not like the others. She's your friend?"

"My best friend," Kaia said.

I hadn't expected the rush of emotion I'd get hearing her call me that. I wondered if the time apart might have made our friendship stronger—we were on a different footing now, maybe one that was more equal. Lev was still shaking his head at what I'd told him. I guess he never thought I'd be capable of this. I couldn't blame him; a few weeks ago, I wouldn't have been.

"Where's Mae? And Noah?" I asked.

Kaia pointed to Mae. She was sitting in the shade of a lean-to, recovering from what must have been a challenging journey. "Noah's there, with his children," Jacob said.

I thought Jacob meant the Underlanders, but they were huddled under another makeshift canopy. He was pointing in the opposite direction. "Nadia and the twins have grown up without him. They thought they'd never see him again." As if on cue, a deep, gravelly laugh rang out. It was hard to believe the sound came from the male I'd met in the Underland.

"Noah," Jacob called. "Look who's here!"

Noah frowned looking at me and walked over. "She's the one who wanted to help."

I'd been outside for only a few minutes, but already the sun's sting was giving me a headache. I put a hand to my forehead where it felt like needles were piercing my skin.

I looked around at Kaia, Lev, Jacob, and Noah and then at the dome. Would they be willing to help me? I licked my lips. The air ripped the moisture away. I couldn't stay in the sun much longer. "I came outside because I need your help. The Underland tunnels have destroyed the City's foundation. And now the lake," my eyes drifted towards it. "With so little to support it, the dome could collapse."

Noah scoffed. "We're not rescuing City people." He spat on the ground at my feet and walked away.

Jacob looked at the dome. In the sunlight it glinted, each panel flashing. "Our mission has been a success. We got what we came for. We're going back to the Mountain."

His words were a kick to my stomach. "Then everyone, all the Citizens will die. They'll be crushed when the dome collapses. Do you want their deaths on your conscience?"

He turned on me. "Conscience? Who are you to tell me about conscience? Do you know what the City took from me? The years with my children that were stolen from me?" he broke off and took a breath. He trembled with anger. "You know nothing."

I wanted to back down, go to the dome, climb the ladder, and hide in my dwelling. But I'd come too far. Mika, Dex and Avi—all the Citizens whether they knew it or not—were counting on me. "We know nothing because we were told nothing. The Council kept us in the dark. We want to help. We want a different City."

"No, you don't. None of you do. You want to keep living in comfort and safety, ignoring what's going on under your noses." I shook my head. He was wrong. "There is a group of people inside who want change. I promise you that. But it won't happen if the dome collapses."

Jacob was unmoved. His eyes were cold when he turned to Kaia. "What will you do?"

Kaia looked at Noah's departing back and at Jacob. "I understand Noah's bitterness, yours too. You were both prisoners for so long. But I was raised as a Citizen. There are people in there I care about." A small thrill of victory ran through me. "But Jacob's right. The things the City has done," she shook her head. "It's built on cruelty. I know it wasn't always. Mae's told me about the early days when the Council had good intentions. But the worst of human nature took over and look where we are."

"We can get the City back to what it was," I said.

Kaia looked doubtful. "Let the CORE figure it out. Come to the Mountain with Lev and me. Start a new life."

I shook my head. A lot of things were unclear to me, but one thing I knew: I wasn't meant for the Mountain. Kaia's life lay outside, with her family, but mine didn't. "I'm not meant for the Mountain," I told her. "My future is in the City. We can remake what the Council's corruption has destroyed."

I saw the skepticism in Kaia's eyes. "I hope you're right." She grabbed my finger and held it up. "Until these are gone, nothing will change." For the first time, I realized there was a small scar where her pulse point had once been. That was where the control had begun, so maybe getting rid of pulse point was where it would end.

I rubbed my thumb over the small bump on my finger. Would Citizens agree?

The wind picked up again, stirring up ripples in the water, reminding me of everything that was at stake.

A thunderous cracking noise ripped through the air. Every Prim froze on high alert. When the next one sounded, I knew exactly what it was.

The dome was falling.

Ama

"Ama?" Luken flew at me, burying his head in my lap. "Are there quakes out here too?"

I held him to me and looked around. The noise wasn't like a quake and the ground wasn't moving. But it made my breath catch in my throat. "It's coming from the City," Kibo said.

He was right. It wasn't the ground at all.

"Unders, you need to be ready to move. We can't stay here any longer," Jacob crouched down and looked at us. "The sun will hurt, so cover yourselves as best you can. Mara will bring extra clothes for you. Wrap your skin and shield your eyes."

"We're leaving?" I asked.

"The dome's gonna collapse."

I frowned in confusion. "How's that big thing gonna come down?"

"The same way the pit did," Lila said. "Isn't that right?" she asked Jacob.

"Something like that."

"And all the City people? Are they getting out like us?"

"That's not our concern." Jacob's eyes were hard when they looked at me. The way I imagined Old Father's would be.

I didn't budge, so no one did. I wanted to know what was going to happen. Jacob looked at me impatiently. "They'll be trapped. Lots will die. Is that what you want to know? It's their own fault. The tunnels weakened the ground and now the dome might fall. All the water that's dammed up is too heavy. They did it to themselves, so don't feel bad."

"We were the diggers," I said.

"Because the City made you work for them, Ama. You had no choice."

I looked at Jacob. His time outside had changed him. Made him harder than when he'd been inside—at least in some ways. Were we going to get like that?

I pressed with another question. Knowing all of those City people were going to feel the fear of a cave-in didn't sit right. "*Can* the City people get out?"

Jacob took a deep breath, like a *mah*, to be patient. "I don't know."

I peeked out from under the canopy again. Prims stood in small groups, packing up or talking. There was one group standing together having a serious discussion. Their hands were waving and they looked worried. One of them was familiar. "It's Sari!" I said. "What's she doing here?" I looked at Jacob.

He had that look that told me he didn't want to say. But he also knew I'd just keep staring at him till he did. "They want you to help dig a trench. It'll ease the pressure on the dam." His voice came out growly and irritated.

I frowned, making sense of things. "So all we gotta do is dig?" I looked at the Unders sitting all around me. I had Romi on one side, like always, and Kibo not too far away. "We know how to do that."

"You'd be helping the people who imprisoned you," he said.

I looked at the dome and imagined what it would sound like when it came crashing down. The sound of a cave-in was terrifying. It stuck in our heads and woke us up with nightmares. We'd left the Underland to get away from those sounds. I didn't want them chasing us outside too.

I squinted into the brightness and saw Sari walking towards us. Already, her pale, shimmery skin was turning pink from the sun. "Can I talk to them?" she asked Jacob.

"I'm not their keeper," he said, gruffly.

"Ama?" Sari called. She ducked under the canopy. A few Unders moved aside to make room for her. She looked at all of us the same way she had when we were in the Underland. "How are you doing?"

I shrugged. Here we were, all squished together and worried about what came next. Sari seemed to understand. "Not what you expected?" she guessed.

"Jacob made it sound different," was all I said.

She nodded, but something else was on her mind. I saw it in the way her eyebrows scrunched up. "I need to ask you something," she started.

"About the digging?" I asked. "Jacob told us."

She gave me a long look. "The City's going to collapse. The only way to save the people inside is to dig a trench to move the water. I know we have no right to ask for your help. Not after everything the City did, but we're not all like that. The way the City used to run is over."

"That doesn't fix the past," Jacob said.

"I know," Sari said, turning to him. "Nothing can. I don't know if there's anything the Citizens can do to make up for what was taken from you." She was talking to Jacob, but to all of us too.

"What got taken?" Luken whispered to Romi. Romi shushed him so she could listen. I guess it was another one of Big Mother's blessings that he'd never know the truth about the Underland. All the things Krux did to keep us trapped—not unless we told him.

Sari stood. "I have to get back. We're trying to evacuate the City and get out as many people as we can." She sighed. "And then, there's the trench. Good luck on the Mountain," she said and turned to go.

"Wait!" I called out. As she'd been talking, I'd imagined all us Unders walking away with the crumbling City behind us. I didn't know if that was what I wanted following us to a new life.

Jacob's eyes were on me and I knew what I was going to say would be hard for him to understand. "I don't think I can go to the Mountain knowing people are in danger, no matter who they are." All the Unders were listening to me again, so I put it another way. "When we're digging in a tunnel, there's no way forward unless we can go back. The rock ahead of us isn't as important as the tunnel behind, otherwise we'll get stuck. If I want to move forward, I need to make sure I'm okay with what's behind me."

Jacob grunted. "What are you saying?"

"I want to help them."

Sari blinked at me. She looked as surprised as Jacob was disappointed. "You're sure that's what you want to do?"

"Sari wasn't the one keeping me in the Underland. She tried to help us. I'm returning the favour. And she's not telling, she's asking. There's a difference."

Jacob gave Sari a hard, distrustful look. He wasn't going to budge on helping the City and I didn't blame him. But I was my own person and for the first time in my life, I could decide what I wanted to do.

Sari

There was a line of us shovelling. Me, then Kaia and Lev. Further on was Ama and a few other Underlanders. The day had turned cloudy, so for the time being, we didn't have to worry about the heat and burn of the sun. I wasn't used to the outside or the work. My body ached and my hands were blistered, but I tried not to think about it; our task was too important.

The Prims stayed in the lean-to shelters watching us. None of them looked eager to help, but they weren't leaving either. "Are they waiting to watch us fail?" I asked Kaia. I didn't like having an audience.

"It's a long walk to the base of the Mountain," Kaia explained. "They won't get there before dark. They'll wait until morning. Plus, the Underlanders won't leave without Ama and the others. Some of the younguns will need help, so the plan is to go all together."

"Then they should help us," I grumbled. "It'll mean they can leave sooner."

Kaia shot me a warning look.

"I know, I know. I wouldn't want to help us either if I were them."

But Lev was feeling as frustrated as I was. "This could take days," he said, jabbing his shovel into the ground and resting his elbow on it. He needed frequent breaks and looked winded after only a few minutes of work, but he insisted on helping, so neither Kaia nor I argued. "Weeks, maybe." With so few of us, he was right. From where we stood, the City stretched into the distance. "It's impossible."

"Sari!" someone called to me. I looked up, grateful for a reason to take a break.

"Mika!" I shouted. I dropped the shovel and went to her. She was wearing a survival suit that covered her completely. Behind her were more Citizens, all of them wearing the white suits. "We used the MAP to find one of the exits," she said. "And a storeroom with supplies. There aren't enough survival suits for everyone, but we can take turns wearing them." She passed one to me. "More shovels too, from the garden sheds." Citizens streamed out of the exit. Lots carried shovels, and other supplies too. Sheets and poles to make shelters, gourds for water, food, and first-aid kits. All the Citizens who had come out with her eyed the valley in front of them anxiously.

With all of us working together, the trench went faster. Stronger diggers made the first path, breaking the parched ground with spades, then the people behind dug out the looser, gravelly dirt. We worked in shifts, taking breaks under the tents; there weren't enough shovels for everyone anyway. While we rested, elders and those that couldn't dig tended our wounds, wrapping our hands so the blisters didn't get infected, which was our biggest concern. Kaia's birth elder explained that after living in the City for so long, our bodies had lost their immunity. A small thing like an infected blister could be deadly.

A separate tent to prepare and serve food was set up. The Underlanders had looked at what was served with a mixture of wariness and wonder.

"That's a carrot," I heard Dex tell one of them. "And this is mint."

By late afternoon, most of the City had been evacuated. There were some people who refused to leave. Even when it was explained that the dome could collapse, they'd resisted. Their fear of Prims and the outside was too great.

The Councillors were getting a taste of the outside, albeit guarded by overseers loyal to the CORE. Ren was being held with them and I avoided looking in his direction. Yulim had stitched his wound and wrapped it in a bandage. I didn't know if he'd survive the outside, or if I wanted him to. I hated him for the danger he'd put us in.

"Who knew there were so many Citizens in the CORE," Mika said with a laugh. She and I were together under the shelter, resting. I'd passed my shovel off to Avi. He must have felt my eyes on him. He turned and grinned at me from his spot along the trench. The sun had started to set and the clouds had moved away. The valley was bathed in warm light. It didn't bite the way I knew it could, but my skin still stung from its first taste of outside. I'd refused a survival suit, arguing that other people needed them more than I did. "Can you believe it? If we'd known there were so many Citizens against the Council, we could have rebelled a long time ago."

"We're not rebelling, we're fixing," I said. "Making the City better and stronger."

"Like a fortress?" Jacob's voice cut into our conversation. I hadn't realized he was listening.

"No," I said, sharply, looking at him. "Those days are done. The Council is done. No one will follow them now. The fear they held over us is gone, so their power is gone."

"It's not going to be that easy," Jacob said. "Tar and the other Councillors won't just give up."

"They won't have a choice. Look at everyone." A few more Prims had decided to help dig. The faster the trench was finished, the sooner they could go home. But Jacob still refused. So did Noah. "There's no going back to how it used to be." Seeing everyone cooperating gave me hope. With time, maybe the Underlanders and Prims could learn to trust us again. It would mean work on our part, redefining who we were, but with the right leaders, anything was possible.

Mika went to find Dex as Noah arrived; he'd been keeping an eye on the Underlanders, making sure they were fed and comfortable.

"Ah," Noah groaned as he sat down. "Feels so good to breathe fresh air again."

Jacob slapped him on the back and turned back to looking at the trench. "Think it'll work?" he asked. I didn't know he was speaking to me until I felt his gaze.

"The engineers are hopeful." Mika was in charge of them. They didn't dig but supervised the path of the trench.

"And if the City stays standing, what then? Will things go back to how they used to be?"

"No," I said with confidence. "They can't because we're not the same."

"You sure about that?" He was staring at the lean-to where the Councillors and Ren sat squished together under guard.

For the moment, Ren was wounded and no danger. He lay off to the side, by himself. But Tar, she needed to know that her days of leading the City were over. I just needed to work up the courage to tell her.

⌒

We worked until the dark made it impossible. Some of the Underlanders had brought their headlamps with them, but after digging for hours, we all needed a rest.

I quickly discovered that sleeping outside was impossible. It wasn't just the hard ground, noises kept me alert. Insects buzzing, people snoring, and the constant creaks of the dome set me on edge. It was a relief when dawn broke.

The sleepless night had given me the chance to do one thing: decide what to say to Tar.

"Where are you going?" Mika asked as I stood up. A few other people, mostly Prims, were moving around. One had collected scraps of wood in a pile and was rubbing two sticks together. I had no idea why. Prim behavior was still a mystery to me.

"I need to talk to someone," I said.

"Who?"

I hesitated before answering. "Tar," I whispered.

Mika sat up, instantly alert. "Why?"

It was hard to explain, but part of it was because of Ama. She was helping so she could move forward feeling at peace with what was behind her. "There's things I need to tell her."

"Now?" Mika asked.

I nodded definitively.

"Do you want me to go with you?" Mika asked. Beside her, Dex inhaled deeply. He hadn't had any trouble sleeping outside.

"No. This I need to do on my own."

Tar and all the Councillors lay on the ground. Blankets had

been doled out last night but there weren't enough for everyone. Like the rest of us, they'd had to share.

Overseers loyal to the CORE guarded the Councillors and Ren. Not that there was anywhere for them to go. The expanse of outside was as much a prison to them as a cell would have been. "I need to speak to"—I was about to say 'Councillor' but stopped myself—"Tar."

The guard nodded and let me pass.

"Hello," I said. "Sleep well?" Her scarlet robe was dusty and her lips dry and cracked.

"What do you want?" she asked. Her words were clipped and laced with disdain.

I crouched down so we were eye to eye. "I've been thinking about something you said when I came to you. You told me my moral ambiguity made us the same." I paused, thoughtful. "And you're right. In some ways, it does. I can make tough decisions. But unlike you, I know right from wrong. If the roles were reversed and it was me sitting here, you'd have me balanced." I leaned back on my heels. "But we're not doing that. Our vision for a City isn't about keeping secrets and hoarding power. We're going to do things differently. You tried to take away everything that mattered to me, Lev, and Kaia, but look at what happened. I got it all back. And then some."

I sat back and looked at her. Her hateful expression stayed the same. "It won't work," she scoffed. "The Citizens need to be controlled."

"I don't think that's true. Maintaining order is one thing, control through fear is...primitive." I stood up, pleased with my word choice, and looked down at her. "As soon as we can, we'll get you a new tunic. One the same as ours. Your days in scarlet are over."

Digging resumed and we were making progress meeting the trench to the stream. I found a spot near Kaia.

We dug for a while before I got up the courage to ask her a question that had plagued me for days. I rested my cheek against the handle of the shovel and looked at Kaia. "I need to ask you something, but you don't have to answer if you don't want to." I took a breath. "Did you and Lev leave together? Was it all part of a plan?"

Kaia stared at me in stunned silence. "No," she said. "I would never have wanted Lev to follow me. When I left, it was, well—" she sighed. "It was out of desperation and pain. I was so hurt."

"I never meant—" Kaia held up a hand to stop me. We were past words of apology.

"Tar manipulated you. The same way she did Lev and me." She shook her head regretfully. "I keep thinking that maybe all of this happened for a reason. Maybe in the end, your decision to match with Lev and my leaving is what set all of this in motion."

I looked at the people digging, sharing water gourds, and talking to each other. There was still a wariness, but there wasn't fear. More and more Prims and Underlanders were joining in. It was easy for me to say the differences that kept us apart stopped mattering when we were digging, but I don't know if that was true. I couldn't speak for the Unders or the Prims. They had both been mistreated by us. But working side by side, it felt like we were forging a new path. A better path because we were all on it together. The Citizens had a lot of work to do. It might take generations, but if we were willing to listen and learn, we could find our way.

"Anyway, you redeemed yourself when you rescued Mae. I'll never forget that you risked your life for her."

A cheer rose up from the diggers on the trench. It had taken a day and a night, but the trench was finished. It joined up with

the stream bed on the other side of the dome. But now was the
real test. Would the trench relieve the pressure from the weight
of the water on the City's foundation?

The only way to find out was to remove the dam, piece by piece.

We held our breath as engineers and Prims worked together
to pry the timbers away. They pulled the top ones off first, pass-
ing them off to the side. The water flowed over the remains of
the dam and then, finding its way free, surged forward. "The
trench is working," Jacob said.

Mika nodded. "I think so," she said. I reached for her hand.
Kaia stood on my other side.

The water was like us. It was finding a new path, a better, safer
path. All of us working together had made it happen.

Ama

E ven after so many sleeps outside, the Prims didn't understand
why we'd pick a cave for our home. They offered to build us
shelters like theirs, but none of us Unders wanted to be apart.
After sleeping together in the pit our whole lives, the last thing
we wanted was walls between us.

Besides, the cave was warm with a fire in the middle of it.
We'd carved out a space for Big Mother. What was left of her was
tucked in there and we visited it anytime we needed to. It was as
good as being in the pit, with better sleeping mats and food. None
of the Prims grumbled about sharing with us, but some looked at
us with pity. Like they were sorry for what we had gone through.

Jacob came to visit almost every day. He'd wander down the
Mountain to sit with us to see how we were getting on. Sometimes
Kaia came too, and then kept walking down the Mountain to
visit the City. That's how it was now. No one was hidden from
anyone else. Sari and her friends looked after the City people,

the Prims looked after their people, and us Unders, well, I guess I was in charge.

"Hey, Ama," Luken said sleepily one night after I'd finished a story. His head was in my lap and Romi was sitting beside me, resting her head on my shoulder. I could see the trees through the cave entrance. They were tall just like Jacob had explained. But there were young ones too. Saplings, he said. Their thin trunks were the hardest to break because they bent. "If we're not living in the Underland anymore, that means we're not Unders." I hadn't thought about that, but he was right.

"So who are we?"

Through the trees, I could the night sky, almost as dark as the pit. But in all that darkness, there were stars twinkling. Lighting up the night and their sparkle took my breath away. There was so much new to discover in this bright world; it gave me a shiver of excitement. "Guess we get to decide that for ourselves."

Sari

Avi stood with me at the top of the spiral staircase. We were looking out over the City, pleased with what we saw. It had been months since the day the City almost fell. The interim tribunal had kept things organized, easing the transition away from a Council. Avi and I were both on it. Everyone who wanted one had a say in how the City should be run. Meetings were held in the open. There were no more secrets.

There was no more energy, either, which was a problem the tribunal had to solve. Our first order of business had been to disable pulse points. We had to show Citizens that there could be another way. It had thrown things into disarray at first, but we had the necessities of food, water, and shelter. If the Prims could live this way, so could we.

The market was busy. More and more Prims made the trip down the Mountain to trade their goods with us. Kaia's brother, Sepp, had a crowd around his stall. Everyone wanted his carvings to decorate their dwellings.

"I got the report from the engineers," Avi said. "They've got a plan."

"For the tunnels?" I asked.

He nodded. "It'll take months, maybe longer to make it safe again."

"The dome has held so far," I said. The trees the Prims had felled for the dam had been lashed together into a scaffold to support the dome underground. It was amazing what could be accomplished when we worked together.

Avi took my hand and together we walked down the spiral staircase. Some days, I thought about the life we'd left behind and got nostalgic. Not because it had been perfect, but it had been innocent, or maybe ignorant was a better word. It was before I'd had to vote on what to do with Ren, Tar, and the other Councillors. Before I'd had a hand in their sentences.

Running a City and caring for the Citizens was a lot of work. I understood now how easy it was for corruption to take hold. But we were determined that our City be different. We'd learned from our mistakes. We knew how to make it better.

"There's Mika," I said and pointed to my sister walking towards us. Dex was beside her, but her distinctive waddle made her easy to spot. The baby was due soon and would be one of the first born in the New City. There would be no pulse point implanted, no communication device behind her ear. Their baby would be the first of a new generation. She would carry the knowledge of many people: Citizen, Underlander, and Prim. All of them together would play a role in her future, but she would have the freedom to create her own path.

Acknowledgements

We would like to thank Catharina de Bakker for being an excellent editor and supporter of our many character and storyline changes, Mel for her behind the scenes work and Sam for working their marketing magic. You are a great team to be part of!

Of course, *Underland* would still be a figment of our collective imagination if not for the support of readers who enjoyed *Pulse Point*. Special shout-out to Mandy Connell, Joanne Kelly and Helen Kubiw for their encouragement to write a sequel.

Finally, thank you to our families: Sheldon, Hart; James and Thomas; Mitchell, Shane, Talia and Casey.